"Arthur Yap's prose indeed has his hallmark blend of simplicity yet sharpness, and the nonchalance sitting oddly astride a self-consciousness in the storytelling often throws up delightful turns of phrases to surprise the reader. Yet this is hardly the point. One might not read Arthur Yap's short stories to seek quite the crispness and density of language as in his poetry, for the prose affords more room for insight into the internal logic of human behaviour and a pristine and loving characterisation of a Singapore long left behind us."

— Toh Hsien Min, poet and editor of *The Quarterly Literary Review of Singapore*

"The qualities one admires in his verse shine brightly in his "flash fiction", too—strikingly modern and unwavering in its commitment to finding out how things behave. He's the David Attenborough of human psychology: he embraces all with their attendant foibles but won't hesitate to dissect each and every one like a top surgeon. Amazingly, he achieves all this without a didactic word. Everyone can learn from Arthur Yap's piquant stories. Such vast wisdom resides in these pared-down lines."

— Yeow Kai Chai, author of *Pretend I'm Not Here*

"The cultural milieu presented in Arthur Yap's stories, with sympathetic if unillusioned insight, is primarily that of the Chinese diaspora, but one that is capable of rapid evolution and voracious assimilation, leading to a kind of utopian forward-directedness, positing the Singapore that is yet to come, and themselves committed to bringing that new society into being."

— Stephen Clark, Professor of English Literature, University of Tokyo

T0083576

NOON AT FIVE O'CLOCK:

THE COLLECTED SHORT STORIES OF ARTHUR YAP

NOON AT FIVE O'CLOCK:

THE COLLECTED SHORT STORIES OF ARTHUR YAP

EDITED BY ANGUS WHITEHEAD

WITH A FOREWORD BY RAJEEV PATKE
AND AN ESSAY BY SHIRLEY GEOK-LIN LIM

NUS PRESS
SINGAPORE

Published by:
NUS PRESS
National University of Singapore
AS3-01-02, 3 Arts Link, Singapore 117569

Fax: (65) 6774-0652
E-mail: nusbooks@nus.edu.sg
Website: http://www.nus.edu.sg/nuspress

ISBN 978-9971-69-791-4 (paperback)

National Library Board, Singapore Cataloguing-in-Publication Data

Yap, Arthur.
    "Noon at Five O'Clock" : the short stories of Arthur Yap / edited by
    Angus Whitehead. – Singapore : NUS Press, [2014]
    89 pages, 216 x 140mm

    I. Whitehead, Angus. II. Title.
    PR9570.S53
    S823 -- dc23   OCN865052557

Front Image: Painting by Arthur Yap. "Untitled", Acrylic on Canvas, 76 x 58.5cm
          (1980s). Courtesy of Ho Chee Lick.
Designed and typeset by: Sarah and Schooling
Printed by: Mainland Press Pte Ltd

With the Support of:

NATIONAL ARTS COUNCIL
SINGAPORE

In memory of Arthur Yap

叶纬雄

1943 – 2006

CONTENTS

BEING A WRITER is not quite the same thing as being a poet, a dramatist, or a fictionist. When the creative impulse can sidestep genre and elide convention, writing declares itself attentive to the naked interface between language and perception where words and experiences try to shape one another in a context relatively—though of course never completely—bare of preconceptions. The resulting tension, if sustained rather than domesticated, retains a sense of newness untamed by tradition. That is how Arthur Yap wrote, at least at the times—rare enough—when neither paint nor poetry seemed apt or sufficient.

The Welsh writer Robert Graves once remarked that a cool web of language winds us in. Words help us forget how hot the day is; they protect our eyes from the dazzle of how red roses can be. Words, words, words, Hamlet exclaimed, only half-feigning disgust and madness. When language becomes soiled currency, and telling stories becomes just another way of telling lies to ourselves, then there is need for something else. It is indeed a need for experimental writing, provided we buy into the conviction that for some writers, all writing is an experiment. That something, which abides in the continuous present tense of an experiment, is often misunderstood as novelty, or given more pretentious names such as originality or truth-telling. That something—of which Yap's work partakes—may be better understood if we think of the time, place, and act of writing as arriving continually at different intersections between silence and speech, between the need to say a lot and the need not to say anything much, the desire to pose life as a question to which all our arts and devices propose responses in the form of answers.

This is an old idea, and it may even sound like an odd idea. It occurs in many times and places: the German writers Novalis and Walter Benjamin; the Irish poet Paul Muldoon. We can assimilate Yap's work to the idea of writing as a kind of problem-solving. We will then read the prose collected here as if it were a series of speculative attempts to formulate questions whose nature we are to guess from reading the prose, as if it were the seen answers to questions that remain unseen, as if it were a set of provisional solutions to problems whose nature we can only guess at from the contours, tone, and direction of the prose in our hands. It is not the answers that should interest us as much as the questions they imply.

Yap approached depth by keeping his eye close to surfaces. He heard inner voices by listening attentively, almost like a mimic, to the nuances of the spoken voice, its idioms and idiolects, the gaps and silences woven into the warp and woof of ordinariness. That much is shared between his poems and the prose collected here. Where these attempts differ from his poems is in how they work at what the English poet John Dryden called the "other harmony of prose". It would be a truism, but a tame rather than a brave one, to say that Yap was among the most remarkable writers to have used English in the last half century, not just in Singapore, but in all the regions and peoples that go under the umbrella notion of "Asia".

He used language—not just English, but certainly English—as if it was a second language, as it was. He made speech sound awkward and difficult. His writing was like a report of the evidence for how words and thoughts, or words and feelings do not always come into the world of utterance harmoniously, or at ease with one another. Not being native to the shapes and sounds of English gives his work a form of estrangement that is salutary and tonic, if we think of all the many writers—from all over the world—who now use English with a fluency, ease and volubility that becomes self-defeating because it has no sense of tension, unease, disquiet, or discomfort.

Yap's writing pulls us up short. It is sparing and bare, like Samuel Beckett's. It is dry like a good martini. It is laconic, like a good joke, all the more delectable for not being too obvious. Above all, it appears or seems—like Arthur himself—shy, reticent, diffident, self-deprecatory, unassuming. But that should not fool you, if you read the writing carefully. It is anything but self-effacing. Rather, it is bold. It is chancy. In a poem called "Alexander's Feast", Dryden declared that "none but the brave deserve the fair". The work collected here is, in a specific sense, brave. It knows fear; it takes risks. It gets where it does even when not quite sure where it wants to go. And it understands the virtue of the dictum "less is more". It is minimalist *avant la lettre*. If you think you know the Singapore of the period from the 1960s to the 1980s, allow this work to catch you a little by surprise. If you are a stranger to that Singapore, allow the work to insinuate the questions it faced for which it essays itself as answers. Take up the challenge as an opportunity. Read these odd little stories. Then wonder what made him write them. What was he getting at, that we, in our prose lives, could be getting at too, but in our own way?

Rajeev S. Patke, Singapore, August 2013
Yale-NUS College

Arthur Yap at Fountains Abbey, Ripon, North Yorkshire, UK, 1973.
Photo credit: Jenny Yap

THIS BOOK INCLUDES all of Arthur Yap's published short stories. Three of these eight stories were included in Robert Yeo's *Singapore Short Stories* (1978) and reprinted several times subsequently, most recently by Pearson Longman in 2002. The remaining five stories, originally appearing in less well-known anthologies and journals, had been by the time of Yap's death in 2006 to a large extent forgotten.[1]

In 2009, I went in search of Yap's early poems in the National Institute of Education's journal collection. In the process, I first encountered his three early short stories written as an undergraduate (or perhaps as a St Andrews' schoolboy)—"Noon at Five O'Clock", "A 5-Year Plan" and "A Silly Little Story"—and published in the early 1960s in *Focus*, the magazine of the literary society of the University of Singapore. These finely crafted, clever, seemingly plotless stories, of whose existence I had been hitherto unaware (no Yap scholar had even mentioned them), were a revelation to me.

Introduced to Jenny Yap in May 2009, I suggested that Arthur Yap's seemingly overlooked, and certainly critically neglected, short stories should be collected in one volume. I thought it might complement the already commissioned collected poems then being edited by Irving Goh. Miss Yap generously agreed to such a short story collection and Paul Kratoska of NUS Press expressed interest in publishing it.

But I had by then only traced six stories. Thankfully, two more were quickly traced through a careful search of the NIE Library's impressive, if underutilised, collection of local literature. These were "Soo Meng", Yap's contribution to Edwin Thumboo's anthology *The Flowering Tree* (1970), and "A Beginning and a Middle Without an Ending", published much later in SKOOB Books' anthology *S.E. Asia Writes Back!* (1993). Only later did I discover that "A Beginning" had been first published over a decade earlier in the Malaysian journal *Tenggara*. In this collection, the subtly reworked 1993 version has been reprinted with significant textual variants recorded in the

---

[1] Such amnesia may explain Robert Yeo's inclusion of the later story "A Beginning and a Middle Without an Ending" in his recent anthology *One—The Anthology* (Marshall Cavendish, 2012), while Rajeev Patke, another re-discoverer and enthusiast of Yap's early short stories, includes "Noon at Five O'Clock" in his coedited *Southeast Asian Writing in English: A Thematic Anthology* (National Library Board, 2012).

notes. In the rest of the stories I have taken the decision to retain the texts as they respectively appeared on their first appearance in print. While in places it might appear that either Yap or the printer has made a grammatical error, it is well to recall this early Singaporean writer's mischievous delight in satirically deploying mimicry of middle-class Singaporean malapropisms made while aspiring to (supposedly) good English. I leave it to the reader to decide whether the stories' "ungrammatical" instances reveal error or informed naughtiness.

I include one other prose piece by Arthur Yap, originally appearing in publications now difficult to locate. Yap's chapter on the local short story from his 1970 pamphlet *A brief critical survey of prose writings in Singapore and Malaysia* is a short but uniquely perceptive essay that deserves to be reprinted. The volume concludes with a brief and inevitably incomplete— but I hope informative—chronology of Yap's life including details of Yap's work as artist, poet and prose writer. This is set against a backdrop of significant political and social events that happened in Singapore during his lifetime. I also include a list of articles on, and mentions of, Arthur Yap in the press and elsewhere (1965–2009). As I say, both chronology and list of publications are almost definitely incomplete. I would be extremely grateful for any corrections, additions and suggestions. Please do email me at whitehead65_99@yahoo.co.uk should you have any such.

In editing the creative work of a skilled linguist in a country that has often privileged language over literature, I have (some might think perversely) brought a contextual rather than a solely textual approach to editing and annotating Yap's stories. Regardless of the high pressure per square inch we encounter in Arthur Yap's very short stories, it is strikingly clear that these stories could have been conceived and written nowhere other than the uniquely strained space that was Singapore city between 1960 and 1993. To ensure that both the scholarly and general reader have as much historical, local, and social context to draw on as they could wish I have spoken to and corresponded with Yap's friends and family, as well as Singapore's historians. Discreetly informed by such interdisciplinary, microhistorical research, I hope the critical apparatus herein unobtrusively suggests minute personal/sociohistorical particulars that may lie somewhere behind, before or between these stories.

I hope this collection of Arthur Yap's long overlooked short stories will intrigue and entertain a new generation of Singaporean and non-Singaporean readers, and initiate critical discussion of a hitherto neglected facet of Yap's opus. At the same time, I hope this volume prompts further exploration of Yap's stories, discussions on their place in the increasingly disputed corpus that is the canon of Singaporean writing, and perhaps most importantly, deliberations on Yap's illuminating-troubling literary representations of an ever changing, if only seemingly matter-of-fact, city-state.

ACKNOWLEDGEMENTS

I WOULD LIKE to thank especially Jenny Yap, as well as Paul Kratoska, Peter Schoppert, Christine Chong Ping Yew and all at NUS Press for their enthusiasm and support for this project. The volume is very much the richer for Christine's time, meticulous care, patience and advice. Special thanks to Kevin Tan, biographer of the admirable David Marshall, and Cyril Wong and Yong Yik Ling for bringing my local-historical lens into considerably sharper focus. My busy but generous NIE colleagues Angelia Poon, Joel Gwynne and Patricia Wong took the time to read and discuss minute particulars of both the stories and accompanying notes. Several of my NIE students on the undergraduate "Singapore and the Region in Literature" course (2013–14), particularly Perdana, Daphne, Chin Yee, Edward, Farah, Naeem, and Siva, have shed further light on these so short but so honed and rich stories. Many thanks to Rajeev Patke (who already knew of these stories) and Shirley Geok-lin Lim (who didn't) for contributing so valuably to this collection, while so excitingly extending the conversation in this new area of Arthur Yap scholarship. Thanks to Chee Lick Ho for loaning, and Mohammad Zulfadi Bin Icksan for photographing, the Arthur Yap painting used on the front cover. Lastly, my gratitude, as ever, to Jinat: "without whom..." in *every* sense.

CREDITS

Acknowledgement is made to the following publications in which Yap's short stories first appeared:

Focus, Singapore (1962–4)
The Flowering Tree, Singapore (1970)
Singapore Short Stories, Singapore (1978)
Tenggara, Malaysia (1982)
Skoob Pacifica Anthology No. 1 (1993)

AN INTRODUCTION TO
THE SHORT STORIES OF ARTHUR YAP

WHILE ARTHUR YAP is now indisputably considered one of Singapore's most accomplished and significant poets, such recognition has been slow in coming. Since the early 1960s until his death in 2006, Yap, never a proactive promoter of his own work, was overshadowed by contemporaries such as Edwin Thumboo, Robert Yeo, Kirpal Singh and other more proactively visible local writers with agendas comparatively more aligned to Singapore's nation building policies.[1] While Yap's poetry, and more recently his painting, have now finally received sustained critical attention, it is not so widely known that Yap also wrote a number of short stories, the earliest of which Rajeev Patke and Philip Holden have recently described as "fine performances in the genre of the very short short-story" (58).

This volume brings together for the first time Arthur Yap's published short fiction. At first glance these eight stories may appear slight. Yet as careful readers of his sparse, understated poetry and visual art are keenly aware, in Yap's works things are never quite as they initially appear. As Paul March-Russell reminds us, the short story is "prone to snap and to confound readers' expectations, to delight in its own incompleteness and to resist definition."[2] Close, patient readings of Yap's short stories—often pushing the genre to a brevity that one is inclined to suspect that almost every word potentially possesses the "pressure per square inch" we expect in one of his poems—are likely to prove similarly satisfyingly discombobulating experiences. Indeed Yap's stories, if secondary to his poems, certainly merit a more prominent place in Yap's opus. If his poetry is more representational than his painting (Lim 1993, 184), Yap's stories appear—on first encounter at least—even more realistic. A cursory reading of those stories reveals little of the explicit absence of conventional grammar we encounter in Yap's poems. In many poems ("letter to an employer" for instance) performative wordplay

---

[1] Yap is also recognized as an accomplished painter. During the 1960s to 80s, he staged numerous exhibitions of his abstract paintings both inside and outside Singapore (see Boey Kim Cheng, "'the same tableau, intrinsically still': Arthur Yap, Poet-Painter" in *Common Lines and City Spaces: A Critical Anthology on the Work of Arthur Yap*, edited by W. Gui., Singapore: ISEAS, forthcoming).

[2] Paul March-Russell, *The Short Story: An Introduction* (Edinburgh University Press, 2009), viii.

is partly so overt due to the minimal space within which to embed such performances. In contrast, Yap's ever so slightly longer stories provide scope for the development of more sustained, subtle and ambiguous linguistic display. Beneath their seemingly flat quotidian surfaces, Yap's beguiling stories are often as rich and as enigmatic as the poems. In addition, the near absence of event in these all but plotless stories draws a careful reader's attention to other elements: specifically a subtly knowing deployment of language (notably in grammatical trickery and the sardonic use of seemingly tired standard English vocabulary and phrases) contributing to the stories' ambiguous, perplexing quality.

Between 1962 and 1993, Yap published eight short fictions. It is still to be established whether any other unpublished stories survive in manuscript form. Three published stories, "Noon at Five O'Clock" (1962), "A 5-Year Plan" (1962), and "A Silly Little Story" (1964) were published while Yap was still an undergraduate in the University of Singapore's literary magazine, *Focus*. The stories were written during Singapore's transition from colonial rule (1819) to self rule (1959) and thence to independence from colonial rule and membership of the newly formed Federation of Malaya (1963). These three stories are characterized by, on the one hand, economy and sparseness, and on the other a representational style that on closer inspection is often troublingly non-representational. As in the poems, so in the stories, Yap's subject is "[s]omething about the human condition, and more specifically about the community that I live in [...] since I live in a community I cannot help but reflect aspects of that community" (Sullivan, 10). Yap remains a writer who attempts to "pare down the descriptive bits", articulating himself "in as few words as possible" with the ultimate aim of representing physical environment "sufficiently to give the reader a sense of what one feels, but not at the same time overwhelm the reader in any way" (Brewster, 99).

Yap is certainly interested in locality. As he told Kevin Sullivan "I suppose basically what I write is something which will reflect my environment" (4). Yap's stories consistently focus upon (and therefore privilege) his personal experience and conception of a Singaporean locality. The majority of his short stories reflect the distinctively Chinese, partly traditional, partly modern urban milieu of his Singaporean childhood and early adulthood (1943–69). Here during a period of profound change and transition, especially in later stories such as "None the Wiser" and

"The Story of a Mask", Yap seems to quietly challenge and problematize traditional Chinese Singaporean culture's negotiations and contentions with an ever more present twentieth-century western modernity.

Yap has described how in his writing he focuses on what he is familiar with: Chinese "folkways" in Singapore (Sullivan, 4). Yap was surely aware of the term's early twentieth-century sociological denotation: "habits of the individual and customs of the society which arise from efforts to satisfy needs [t]hen they become regulative for succeeding generations and take on the character of a social force" (Sumner, iv). Yap refers to "folkways" present in pre- and post-war Singapore—whether as "need" or "social force" is not made totally clear—in "The Story of a Mask" (1978). At the moment Yap was writing, many of those folkways had already or were in the process of passing away. "The Story of a Mask" ambivalently explores the initial survival in Singapore of Chinese traditions already expunged in Communist China and their subsequent erosion in the rapidly developing nation state itself post 1965: "They [early to mid-twentieth-century migrants to Singapore from China] brought with them, among other things, their beliefs, their superstitions and folkways".

To explore the traditional folkways of one's own ethnic tradition may seem a rather modest and perhaps exclusionary strategy for a writer in Singapore, a city-state also comprising of Malay, Tamil, Eurasian and other ethnic communities. But Yap grew up surrounded by an urban, almost exclusively monocultural environment; on the one hand the milieu of the upper middle-class, dominantly Chinese neighbourhood of River Valley Road, on the other a less developed but more democratised Chinatown, 1943–70. And it is in this environment that the majority of Yap's stories (as well as many of his poems) are situated. Yap rarely engages with Singapore beyond these neighboring, predominantly Chinese urban spaces. Aside from the brief appearance of the balloon seller in "Soo Meng" (and perhaps the mandore in "Noon at Five O'Clock"), Singapore's Malay, Eurasian and Tamil dimensions are almost invisible. Such a culturally exclusive lens might still seem curious in such an educated and cosmopolitan writer. Yet Yap's consistent exploration of past and present Chinese folkways—that by their nature might imply a traditional, domestic ethnic separation from other races and cultures—seems to resonate tellingly with a Singapore in which the possibilities of creating a Malayan culture through synthesis expressed in the early 1950s rapidly gave way to the harsh reality of a multiracialism that encouraged affiliation to imagined cultural pasts outside of Singapore. Seen in this light, Yap's exploration of his own Singaporean "folkways" becomes tellingly significant.[3]

In any case, it might be argued that Yap's apparently monocultural renderings are comparatively more credible than other Singaporean writers' attempts to ventriloquize ethnic cultures of Singapore other than their own.[4] Nevertheless, our sense of Yap's exploration of local folkways is also complicated by an ambiguity concerning the extent to which Chinese customs and traditions evident in early to mid-twentieth-century Singapore are also identifiably those of the Chinese, but also Anglican, anglophile Arthur Yap. Born during the Japanese occupation and known beyond his university years as "Chioh Hiong", Arthur Yap's first language was "Chinese" (Brewster, 104–5). Yap was thus on the one hand a native of Singapore, grounded in traditional Chinese culture and folkways and thus organically part of a living tradition (something many Chinese Singaporeans including Lee Kuan Yew subsequently struggled to synthetically reconnect with). On the other, Yap deliberately chose English as his language of literary and non-literary communication (Brewster, 104–5), and embraced a range of other aspects of the twentieth-century west, notably its literature and fine art. Yap then brings a far from commonplace, dually informed perspective to bear on twentieth-century Singapore and specifically the minute particulars of its Chinese folkways.

As Chinese but also Anglican-Anglophile Singaporean, Yap appears to be simultaneously participant and "ethnic social observ[er]" (Lim 2009, 176) of this community. In focusing on a specific, initially endangered then synthetically reinforced cultural environment, not unrelated to the author, it could be argued that Yap's stories bear some resemblance to those of mid-twentieth-century short story writers such as Saul Bellow and Isaac Bashevis Singer in their detailed representations of similarly migrant Jewish communities in urban North America. Even in his first, and arguably most

[3] Yet it might be noted that in "A Beginning and a Middle Without an Ending", the last story included in this collection, which presents an imagined near-future Singapore, most of such local, traditional folkways seem to have been fully expunged and replaced by the imported and confected.
[4] The only exceptions I can think of are the short stories of Gregory Nalpon. See *The Wayang at Eight Milestone; Stories and other Writings*, edited by Angus Whitehead (Epigram, 2013).

accomplished, short story, "Noon at Five O'Clock" (1962), published when Yap was just 19, we encounter a committed engagement with not only racially and locally bound folkways but also a celebration of the material survival of the city's colonial past potentially running counter to Singapore's fast-forward privileging of "progress" from the early 1960s onwards.

> There were doors on either side of the tall, grey walls. Part of which walls, plaster has flaked off showing the raw bricks. They were doors typical of old buildings—rather sunken in. He came to the dead end of the lane. The two blocks of building had been blocked by another lying sidewise. Engineers and architects may scheme and "city-plan" but there are always (to him rather delightful) accidents.
>
> —"Noon at Five O'Clock"

While Yap's stories in both content and form (often fragmentary, always brief, oblique) might reveal a resistance to an increasingly conformist contemporary national discourse, it should be recalled that the traditional folkways he portrays are of still identifiably distinct strands in Singapore's racial majority. That sense of difference within an increasingly hegemonised majority is evident in the fact that Cantonese Wong Loo in "A Silly Little Story" can barely communicate with a fellow Chinatown resident and seller of antiques. Yap thus explores the folkways of particular and differentiated, if subsequently glossed and marginalized, ethnic strands within Singapore's majority. To what extent elements of such Chinese Singaporean folkways have survived in some form or even have helped shape the dominant rhetorics and identities that make up the Singaporean modernity so evident twenty years later in Yap's most formally experimental "A Beginning and a Middle Without an Ending" (1982, rev. 1993) is left beguilingly unclear.

One of Yap's other later stories, "The Effect of a Good Dinner", explores match-making in the Chinese community in Singapore, a custom that continued into the 1960s but had began dying out not least due to foreign influences, notably pop culture, which made a younger generation, including Yap, momentarily more autonomous and assertive about their own destinies. The effect of American pop music on a younger Singaporean Chinese generation is explored in the earlier "A Silly Little Story". While Chinese folkways in Singapore from 1965 encountered a "top-down" modernity in the guise of an increasingly authoritarian and interventionist state, from the late 1950s if not earlier, local youth culture, influenced by Western modernity, seems also to have played its part in eating away at Singapore's less legislated familial traditions.

In "None the Wiser", Teng Soo and Mei Ching's discreet, conspiratorial mockery of a wealthier sibling's assumed pretence of an expensive and ugly chandelier may be linked to aesthetic considerations, but is primarily concerned with the object's cost, perhaps provoking *kiasu* rivalry and negativity. Yet the couple's attitude to the ceiling lamp needs also to be read in the context of immediate post-independence era rhetoric. In a speech delivered at the University of Singapore in 1968, Lee Kwan Yew asserted, "Poetry is a luxury we cannot afford". While the extent to which culture remains an inexpedient luxury in Singapore is perhaps debatable, it might also be argued that we encounter in the choice of a hideous and exorbitantly expensive lamp a characteristically Singaporean elision of culture and commodity.

The early stories

When Yap wrote his first short stories in the early 1960s, the genre of the short story in Singapore, while occupying a prominent place in both Chinese and English writing, was still unformed. Published in a local university's literary magazine, Yap's stories must have initially reached, and were perhaps written for, a very small, elite, academic and local readership.[5]

In his 1970 pamphlet, *A Brief Critical Survey of Prose Writings in Singapore and Malaysia*, Yap devotes a brief chapter to the local short story, (reprinted in this collection, *see* page 69) in which he observes, "The 1950s, and particularly the 60s, [saw] the emergence of a greater and more articulate attempt in making the short story more substantial in assimilating the locale and life here" (17). Writing after he had published the first four stories in this volume, Yap's views on the development of the local short story from 1950 to 1970 illuminate his own crafting of short but highly substantial stories. In discussing Tan Hock Seng's "rather elephant-footed" stories, and other local short story writers' "lack of fluency", and "awkwardness in presentation",

---

[5] An undergraduate contemporary of Yap's at the University of Singapore in the early- to mid-1960s, Koh Tai Ann, recalls encountering Yap's early stories in *Focus* and enjoying "their rather enigmatic, spare quality" (pers. comm., 18 November 2009).

Yap concludes: "unless the ideas are either startling or profound enough, it is unlikely that the story can be expected to be borne solely by the weight of the ideas alone" (18).

> On the other hand, Awang Kedua's "A New Sensation" and the stories by Lee Kok Liang are eloquent, and enlist the reader's attention fully. This is due to a greater skill in presentation and in letting the story unfold itself, without having to become turgidly moralistic or to lapse into question begging.
>
> (18, emphasis mine)

Yap goes on to praise Lee's "subtle ring of irony", his "restrained and subtle" and "well-integrated" style, especially in "Ibrahim Something" (18). For Yap, Lee is a writer who "feels and understands his subject matter" (20). Elsewhere Yap praises a now almost wholly forgotten local writer, Choo Soon Yin's "oblique narrative [...] and sureness of touch" (19) in his "skillfully constructed" stories (20). The qualities Yap praises Lee and Choo for, we encounter in abundance in Yap's own eight stories.[6]

Writing almost a decade later, Robert Yeo identified three "categories of short stories commonly written in Singapore": 1) "stories of social realism", 2) "stories of the inner life" and 3) stories that are "part-real, part-allegorical" (118).[7] Although Yap holds a particularly prominent place in Yeo's anthology, as we shall see, it is very difficult to place Yap's stories neatly into any of Yeo's three categories. All three of Yap's early stories share a distinctive feature, atypical of most modern short stories: the complete absence of direct speech.[8] While Yeo also suggests that Singapore's early short story writers represented in his 1978 collection exhibit "no specific influence" (115), Yap's first story suggests one identifiable literary forebear. As a schoolboy at St Andrew's School, Yap read all of D. H. Lawrence's work and was especially captivated by Lawrence's prose (see Sullivan, 3). Lawrence's influence seems evident in the opening of

---

[6] One wonders to what extent Lee Kok Lian and Choo Soon Yin's stories influenced Yap's later stories. Choo's wartime "trio of stories" (19) may have influenced Yap's own later triptych discussed below. In the same chapter, Yap also praises the stories of Lim Beng Hap (19).

[7] Yeo's sole example here is Gregory Nalpon's "The Rose and the Silver Key".

[8] This is curious as according to his friend, fellow student and colleague Koh Tai Ann, Yap was a wickedly expert mimic of colleagues and students (pers. comm., 14 April 2009). Yet direct speech is cleverly deployed in three of the five later stories.

"Noon at Five O'Clock":

> The sun seems to dazzle everything it touches. And however acclimatised, no one can be impervious to its seeping heat. He was going home, and suddenly he felt sick. Perhaps it wasn't very wise to have walked that distance under the noon sun. But this is one of the things one does. Without having to see if it's wise or otherwise, that is.

But what is most distinctive is the way in which throughout this story, common parlance and standard English are utilized for what Lim in another context has described as "syntactically perverse" (137) purposes. For example, on his unsanctioned entering of the rear of a large old shophouse, the schoolboy protagonist first imagines and then quickly dismisses a "helpless", "sprawling maiden" before hopefully anticipating (but failing to encounter) a "bleary-eyed boy". Each hackneyed phrase ("helpless maiden" echoes Walter Scott's description of Rebecca in *Ivanhoe*), may reflect a late 1950s colonial schoolboy's bookishness, but both resonate tellingly as the boy encounters not only the shophouse but also himself.

In his peregrinations, the schoolboy increasingly takes on the role of the flâneur. While the Oxford English Dictionary defines a flâneur as a "[usually pedestrian] lounger or saunterer, an idle 'man about town'", after Walter Benjamin (drawing on Baudelaire) the flâneur has become an emblematic figure of urban, modern experience, notably spectatorship, throwing light not only on nineteenth-century urban class tensions and gender divisions, but also on modern alienation, mass culture, and the postmodern spectatorial gaze.[9] Yet in Singapore, on the eve of independence and further redevelopment, such an attitude and pose of the flâneur must have remained only just possible to maintain in the city's public spaces. Although published in 1962, before Singapore was neither independent nor nation, it is interesting that "Noon at Five O'Clock" represents a schoolboy as an individual, peculiar, idiosyncratic persona, reminiscent of the quietly perverse, potentially subversive, lenses Lim locates in Yap's poetry (Lim

---

[9] *See* Walter Benjamin's "The Return of the Flaneur", *Selected Writings II 1927–1934*, trans. Rodney Livingstone et al., ed. Michael W. Jennings, Howard Eiland, and Gary Smith (Cambridge: Harvard, 1999), 262–7.

1993, 134). Thus in his own mind, the schoolboy diverges from the assumed and invisible owners of the terraced residence he enters: "But sometimes people just live in the front. And leave the back to the family ghosts. And never look back." As the story progresses, via the late-colonial landscape of early 1960s Singapore city, the schoolboy appears to travel back in time, ultimately discovering the personally significant by penetrating a hidden, and seemingly deserted interior past. The story can be read as an affirmation of the personal, individual, and private in the context of the increasing incursion and prevalence of collective, public, and national concerns on everyday life in Singapore.

In both "A 5-Year Plan" and "A Silly Little Story", wider social commentary, or rather the raising of hard questions, is mediated through the familial-domestic: don't the indebted, ever working, and increasingly deadened couple of "A 5-Year Plan" (1962) gesture to a far wider problem and condition in a progressive Singapore? If in "A Silly Little Story" (1964), Wong Loo "adher[ing] quietly but stoutly to his little area of animation" would indeed have been as happy in the Chinatown of San Francisco as that of Singapore what does this suggest about Singapore's identity as postcolonial Malaysian state, or of the Chinese diaspora generally? What does the insular and undynamic Wong Loo's aversion to Communism reveal about his liking for Singapore, three years after the formation of the Barisan Socialis? Ironically, post-independence and Separation Singapore's policies like Mao's in China would also "greatly disturb [...] Chinese traditions and turn [...] the social order topsy-turvy" (16). Although the narrator describes the "tolerant man" Wong Loo as "an ignorant man" it remains unclear to the reader whether it is the traditional Chinese immigrant Wong Loo or his young, increasingly modern/western sons who is truly ignorant.

"A Silly Little Story" rehearses a dialogue between two generations of Chinese Singaporeans in the early 1960s on the cusp of radical national change. Wong Loo's sons see meaning in American pop songs that they describe as "witty". But Wong Loo,

> In an unreasonable frame of mind, [...] always thought Singapore was a no-man's land: his reasoning was most illogical —Singapore, a Malaysian state; he himself, originally a Chinese, everyone speaks some English; and his unredeemable son hopped about to American pop-songs.

But is Wong Loo's reasoning illogical, his description of Singapore in 1964 unreasonable? To many of the first readers of "A Silly Little Story", Wong Loo's apparently homespun conclusions may have seemed uncannily accurate, tellingly undermining the reasoned, progressive tone of the narrator.

The later stories

During the 17 years following Singapore's expulsion from the Federation of Malaysia on 9 August 1965 and the beginning of the new nation, Arthur Yap published five more stories: "Soo Meng", appeared in Edwin Thumboo's anthology *The Flowering Tree* (1970); "The Story of a Mask", "The Effect of a Good Dinner" and "None the Wiser" were published in Volume One of Robert Yeo's anthology *Singapore Short Stories* (1978) and "A Beginning and a Middle Without an Ending" was first published in the Malaysian literary journal *Tenggara* (1982).[10]

The often near plotless modern short story with its formal potentialities for implication and obliqueness has been described as a "dissident form of communication" (March-Russell, ix, 66). Indeed in these four later stories, Yap continues to utilize much of the linguistic play, undermining of textual authority, and gesturing to social criticism via satire and ambiguity found in the early stories. But, at least in the three stories included in Yeo's collection, Yap also reaches farther into Singapore's past and therefore engages more fully and more exclusively with increasingly threatened and distinctively Chinese Singaporean folkways. With the obscured ambiguities evident in the earlier stories, Yap exhibits ever more complex responses to those folkways and their demise, often reflecting the swift, jarring changes accompanying the ongoing development and identity-forging of the nation state, and thereby quietly questioning the official rhetoric's complacent glossing of the grassroots trauma of aggressive development in 1965–75.

In these stories, Yap prefigures a later generation of writers, who have, as Angelia Poon observes, "[e]schew[ed] bare polemic for more nuanced political commentary [and] offer a view of history and politics often

---

[10] The issue also contained a poem by Yap ("When Last Seen") and four paintings: "A Small Complete View I", "Early Evening", "Landscape Situation II", and "Overland".

through the prism of the personal and the familial" (365). One wonders, despite Yap's writing during a period of pronounced authoritarianism and censorship, could his detached portrayal of the personal and familial reveal Yap deploying a mediated strategy of personal-political expediency?

By titling his 1970 story "Soo Meng", Yap foregrounds a mentally disabled child in a seeming tale of domestic Singapore. Disability becomes an indicator of the extent of Singaporean attitudes at both local and national levels in the second half of the 1960s, a period during which the state unapologetically focused on economic advancement at the expense of social welfare considerations. Careful reading of "Soo Meng" also reveals Yap's understated mimicry of an elite gendered register of Singapore English, as an index of the local-national mindset from which it emanated.[11]

Yap in representing the balloon seller at the conclusion of "Soo Meng" as Indian and taking him out of a fun fair such as the "New World" and into a local neighborhood, touches on an ethnic anxiety in Singapore overshadowed in 1970 by recent, violently manifest Chinese-Malay tensions. Local historian Kevin Tan recalls that in the 1960s, "very young Chinese kids tended to be afraid of [...] Indians" (pers. comm., 2 July 2010). Many Chinese parents of the period used Indians (particularly Sikhs) as a bugaboo to frighten their children into good behavior, telling them, for example that if they did not finish their vegetables they would be kidnapped by Indians. A so-called normal Chinese Singaporean child of the period might therefore have been too frightened to approach the balloon seller alone. Soo Meng's disability is accompanied by numerous unique and attractive qualities, not least a racial colour-blindness and trust, that distinguishes him from his already conditioned peers.

"The Effect of a Good Dinner", "None the Wiser" and "A Story of a Mask" were published and almost certainly written after Yap's postgraduate studies at the University of Leeds, UK (1974-5) before taking up the position of lecturer in linguistics at the University of Singapore. The period of over a year spent away from Singapore in which Yap also spent periods of time in London and Wales, may have contributed to an increasingly detached quality in his prose writing. Taken together, "The Effect of a Good Dinner", "None the Wiser" and "A Story of a Mask" represent what might be described

---

[11] Such mimicry and linguistic mischieviousness is also evident in the later "None the Wiser" and "A Beginning and a Middle without an Ending".

as a post-independence triptych a decade after separation representing the introduction, presence and passing of traditional Chinese folkways in Singapore. While "The Effect of a Good Dinner" and "The Story of a Mask" paint broad pictures encompassing between them almost half a century of Singapore's recent history 1930–78, "None the Wiser", sandwiched between the other two stories and therefore the triptych's centrepiece, could be described as a contemporary and intimately domestic portrait. The stories' shared underlying theme is the gradual, but nevertheless relentless hemorrhaging or wearing away of the inner life and Chinese Singaporean traditions in past and contemporary Singapore. At the beginning of "The Effect of a Good Dinner" the narrator opines, "Custom and heritage are the easiest things to kill; even if they are not killed, they are easily jolted into a hemorrhage". This allusion to "a hemorrhage" foreshadows the climax of "None the Wiser" where, while in a manifest fracturing of traditional filial piety, Mrs Tan's children consider whether to send their mother to a home for the aged, a rain-soaked door sash heavily bleeds its red dye.

In "The Effect of a Good Dinner", Yap, writing in about 1978, might also be suggesting that aspects of the prevalent "modernity" of post-independence Singapore, framed in an official narrative described by Poon as a "forward-looking teleological story of orthodox nationalism and nation-building" (365), derive much from traditional Chinese folkways still surviving in Singapore in the decades preceding independence. Before the Second World War, the narrator's granduncle, negotiating an encroaching modernity, works hard in order to purchase in addition to a traditional Chinese indicator of wealth and prosperity (a jade bangle for his wife), objects redolent of modernity and material prosperity: a portable radio, a bike and a car. But ironically the "quickening effect" of the postwar period leads to the granduncle's desire for a traditionally sanctioned second wife.

While "The Effect of a Good Dinner" explores past, lost Chinese folkways, "None the Wiser" presents contemporary, surviving and arguably more fundamental elements of the tradition threatened by Singaporean modernity, characterized by Lim as a "society organized around self-centred material relations" (Lim, 150). The story is set in the present or near present (i.e., in the midst of Singaporean development during the 1970s). The Tans have moved from their original traditional family "terrace-house" (33) and have dispersed across the rapidly developing island to newer kinds of residences available to the upper and middle class in early postcolonial

Singapore. If the chief characters in "The Effect of a Good Dinner" are representative of their respective pre- and post-wartime generations, in "None the Wiser", Mrs Tan's three siblings' households can perhaps also be read as representative of early postindependence Singapore. The story's title suggests that despite material progress, it is perhaps not so much Mrs Tan, but her children and by implication their entire generation that are "none the wiser".

In "The Story of a Mask" the third and final part of Yap's Singapore triptych, Wong Loo (the protagonist's name and sections of the text are partially recycled and reworked from the earlier "A Silly Little Story"), representative of tradition and modernity, actually becomes a figure of a modern day myth in this ostensibly modern short story about past and contemporary Singapore. Through Yap's narrative experimentation, this modern story reverts to folk tale. Yap in doing so comments not only on the ebbing of traditional folkways but also other aspects of imaginative and cultural life in Singapore. "The Story of a Mask", like "The Effect of a Good Dinner", refers to the period 1930–65 as a past golden age of material and cultural prosperity. Yap thereby problematizes contemporary national rhetoric characterizing Singapore's post-independence era, 1965–78, as a period of unprecedented and uncomplicated progress.

Originally published in 1982, "A Beginning and a Middle Without an Ending" should be read in the context of a Singapore that in many ways has been materially transformed beyond recognition from the Singapore represented in Yap's earlier stories. 1982 marked seventeen years since independence, a decade since the Singapore economy took off, and the period in which Lee Kuan Yew's 1965 prediction of Singapore's transubstantiation from part-swamp part-modern city to metropolis in a decade seemed to have been almost wholly fulfilled. And yet by the early 1980s, almost two decades of government social engineering policies had begun to wear away at the traditional-local community values that had initially survived despite the mandatory national exodus from village and urban neighbourhoods to elite private houses and condominiums or for the majority of Singaporeans, public housing, the ubiquitous "Heartlands" comprising of Housing and Development Board high rise new towns. "A Beginning and a Middle Without an Ending" might almost be read as a wry prophecy, the ultimate logical conclusion to the hemorrhaging of folkways explored in the 1978 triptych.

"A Beginning and a Middle Without an Ending" portrays a sophisticatedly urban, identifiably modern Singapore to the virtual exclusion of the island's traditional local folkways and topography. Nevertheless, the past, present and futuristic milieu seem equally, unmistakeably Singaporean through the presence of both Singlish and bullying, negative and unkind *kiasu* attitudes and actions, suggestive of Singapore's pervasive predatory capitalism. If the reflexively postmodern story lacks plot, it is written in firmly realist prose. Yap presents two snapshots principally of the same Chinese woman's life in Singapore. The first snapshot captures a domestic milieu in the early post independence period, 1969–75; an older sister, Elaine, slaps a younger, Betty, after the latter's emotional rendering of a Mandarin song, culminating in a collapse. The second snapshot takes place "thirty-five years later", from the perspective of the time the story was originally written (1982), an imagined twenty-first century future, about 2004–11. That future vision appears to be based on an imagined trajectory of development extrapolated from then current early 1980s government policies. Yap represents a future city state in which a dubiously qualified elite do not merely fail to assist and sympathise, but also appear to take an almost sadistic pleasure in the disappointment and discomfort they cause, as well as in the power they can exercise, over their subordinates.[12] Yap here appears to delight in capturing in dialogue the malevolently grating 'good' English of Singapore's female elite. Yap's earlier stories often focus upon peculiar characters against a recognizably Singaporean backdrop. In this story, however, Betty, is transformed from an initially idiosyncratic, creative, and aspirational younger sister and victim into a successful, if cruelly pragmatic and discouragingly domineering businesswoman.[13]

The second section of "A Beginning and a Middle Without an Ending" portrays Betty's professional, public life: "Later, thirty-five years later [as] the executive director of a modeling school". In this futuristic, aspirationally chic and incredible Singaporean interior setting, Betty's opposite number, and therefore elect equal, Vicki's hand is described as "a nubile technological extension" of an "elegant white telephone" (76). Betty's

[12] The story seems a poignant complement to the simply nosy but kindly 'kampung spirit' of the earlier Singaporean female milieu represented in "Soo Meng".
[13] One might illuminatingly compare this story with Gregory Nalpon's "Two Faces". *See* Gregory Nalpon, *The Wayang at Eight Milestone* (2013), 70–2.

"eggshell" office denotes not only elite commercial taste, but also a fragility. While we are left to guess what has occurred in the thirty-five years between these two 'snapshots' of contemporary-future Singapore, the temporal context suggests that "A Beginning and a Middle Without an Ending" can be read as a Singaporean national tale related through a privileged female Chinese Singaporean milieu.

Singapore's history beyond the two snapshots presented is either eternal, un-guessable or in a state of stagnation—a cultural, superficial vacuum—unable to mature culturally beyond its current bureaucratic and mass commercial culture.

> An ending must be found. Without it, Betty Wong could only go on rejecting the Zatikas. The Zatikas are abundant. Somewhere in between the rejection and the realization that the Zatikas were being rejected for nothing, for things that weren't there; somehow, in between the chuckle and the choke, Betty Wong drew a conclusion. It was the collapse before the song started. And poor Elaine, the face, the recollection of the face that could not launch Betty Wong's hand.
>
> —"A Beginning and a Middle Without an Ending"

In both cases, in contexts of Chinese Singaporean female education and play, the reworked Marlovian allusion becomes negative. That Betty's face launched Elaine's hand to strike her in youth, while Elaine's face in middle age cannot launch Betty's hand to write a cheque, may suggest Yap making a statement not only about the negative effects of a less than nuanced authoritarianism, but also about a nation motivated by beauty rather than need, changing style and technology for technology's sake over genuine thought, or substance derived from a sustained immersion in art, philosophy and culture.

The story may also comment on the progression of racial/ cultural politics in Singapore during the early 1980s. The narrator observes that Miss Zatika, a rejected nominee for Betty's "Inner Poise and Zen Meditation" course, had "prior to nomination [...] been Au Lin Soo, a healthy fresh-face." But Yap's intention here, if any, is unclear. At first glance it appears as if an aspiring Chinese model attempts to take on a more mature, sophisticated identity. The phrase "meditative mutton", may suggest that the name change indicates a bid by the wannabe model to get into one of Betty's 'transcendent' beauty courses. Has the model, in a bid to be accepted on Betty's Zen meditation course, undergone a radical (perhaps racial-religious) identity change and gone for a more mature and modest look? Or does the name change suggest a switch from modern Chinese Singaporean to another identified culture? Although "Zatika" might superficially resemble a Malay Muslim or Indian name, it is also recognized as a Croatian surname as well as a Basque word meaning "cut into pieces". Is Yap then here making an allusion to one effect of Singapore's multicultural history as well as its modernity, the increasing racial/cultural indeterminacy of Singaporeans in a city-state in which according to each inhabitant's identity card race remains a defining factor? Is the aspirant model Au Lin Soo/Miss Zatika taking on a European, and therefore in this possible future, exotic, international identity while in reality remaining restricted to a South East Asian milieu typified by Betty's imminent show in Manila?

Conclusion

While in Yap's first story "Five O'Clock at Noon" with its almost solipsistic focus upon the artist-protagonist, reflections on Chinese folkways in the context of national modernity are marginal, from Yap's second story "A 5-Year Plan" onwards, those folkways become a primary, abiding concern. In a discussion of Yap's poems, Shirley Lim draws a dichotomy between the poles of good tradition, bad modernization (see Lim 2009, 176). However, in Yap's stories, things are much more ambivalent. In the context of Singapore in the early post-independence era, Yap utilizes embedded ambiguities as a strategy for a mediated exploration of local folkways against the wider background of politically engineered full speed social change. That ambiguity I would argue seems to derive from Yap's ambivalent, not overtly critical, but often seemingly uneasy response to Singapore's relentless progress to modernity. Such a response seems shaped by Yap's own attempts as a cosmopolitan Singaporean man to come to terms with change as it happens, as much as an attempt to negotiate authoritarian censorship. Things are further complicated by a suggestion that problematic elements of modernity in the Singaporean context may have their roots in the survival of arguably 'bad' traditional local folkways.[14] While raising questions about the effects of western-modernity penetrating Singapore from above and below, the stories also interrogate "Asian values" as well as tradition—aspects of which survive— championed by the legislators of the nation state. Taken together these stories represent a telling commentary upon post independence Singapore's selective retention and privileging of aspects of Chinese tradition and a similarly selective acceptance of modernity and western values. In these stories Eastern traditional values are potentially as suspect as Western modern ones. If we accept this rather bleak reading, Yap's character Wong Loo, certainly in his 1962—and perhaps in his 1978—incarnation, is not so much a symbol of traditional Chinese folkways and values, but rather representative of a pragmatically mercantile, Chinese Singaporean sensibility which has bled into Singapore's adaptation of modernity.

Indeed, by 1978, 13 years into the nation-state project, Yap, as short story teller/historian-chronicler, represents not the present but the period c. 1930–60 as a period of prosperity in which folkways, although changing, fading, did not disappear instantly. The period seems to be used as a means of interrogating Singapore's present and future direction during the 1960s and 1970s, a period of considerably accelerated folkway haemorrhage.

Yap is already recognized as a poet whose voice tentatively locates, satirises and subverts an emerging sense of Singaporean nationhood. The aesthetic and ideological trajectories of Yap's prose in many ways resemble those encountered in his poetry. If Yap's eight deceptively simple stories reward careful reading, they also provoke difficult questions. Their condensed, enigmatic and perplexing nature; the rich polysemous nature of apparently mundane but surely painstakingly chosen and placed words and phrases; and the stories' particularly difficult endings, often resemble his poems. In writing prose only superficially resembling (and mischievously parodying) the functional 'good' but clichéd English urged on Singaporeans 1965–80, Yap appears to be quietly deploying linguistic trickery to discreetly subvert and mock the prevalent rhetoric. There is something very curious about Yap in that his stories draw upon very English and redundant uses of the English lexis juxtaposed with very local, quotidian and contemporary usages. If nothing else, Yap displays here a richly eclectic, tolerant, erudite and culturally mature artistic sensibility, derived from a lifelong, genuine

[14] *See* Montague, 142.

immersion in Chinese folkways as well as western art and popular culture that could composedly accommodate both Singapore's colonial/ traditional past and contemporary local modernity—a sensibility that often seems to continue to elude forgers and legislators of the nation-state.

Angus Whitehead

Noon at Five O'Clock

THE SUN SEEMS to dazzle everything it touches. And however acclimatised, no one can be impervious to its seeping heat. He was going home, and suddenly he felt sick. Perhaps it wasn't very wise to have walked that distance under the noon sun. But this is one of the things one does. Without having to see if it's wise or otherwise, that is.

He reached home. No one was in. His father would be at work. Not sweating perhaps. For there must be some air-conditioners around the place. He didn't know where the others were. Then he remembered the amah[1] was in. Anyway, she always is. Being perfectly domesticated by now. He had come home rather flustered.

Lunch-time; she set a plate of rice and some curry on the table, and returned to the kitchen to conjure up something else. The sight of the curry took away his appetite. Somehow he couldn't understand why people take it at most meals. In a hot country! The mandore who "does" the neighbourhood[2] could squat near a drain and cram down rice-and-curry. People are always so logical. So why shouldn't he have something more appealing, to the eye, to the mood. He hated that damn curry. And decided to take a walk. Again, it was perhaps not very wise. But.

He didn't run out of the house. He knew where he might want to go. He knew of people who run out of their houses, and then stood goggle-eyed wondering what to do with themselves next. He went to a bookstore. Not that it was a particularly wonderful place. But it is one of those places where one can look nonchalantly around and be taken as putting on a becoming sceptic attitude. That idea rather humoured him. But he could still feel the confounded heat. He went out.

Sometimes there's really no knowing. He didn't know the side-lane he took could be that pleasant. He did not like it the first fifty feet. There were the industrious S.A.T.A. posters appealing for more blood.[3] He wasn't quite in the mood to give anything. Let alone that. There were also some hawkers. Rather obscure hawkers at that. Somehow they could all sell their wares. To anonymous-loving customers perhaps.

There were doors on either side of the tall, grey walls. Part of which walls, plaster has flaked off showing the raw bricks. They were doors typical of old buildings—rather sunken in. He came to the dead-end of the lane. The two blocks of building had been blocked by another lying sidewise. Engineers and architects may scheme and "city-plan" but there are always (to him rather delightful) accidents. There were several doors on that block leading, to what he thought, might be shop-houses or coffee-shops. He didn't want to turn back. And chose the oldest and creakiest-looking door. It would lead him to, or rather through, the oldest and creakiest coffee-shop. He thought. And being the oldest, the proprietor would naturally have nothing to be proud of. Therefore he could pass through without having to "drink" anything. The door groaned miserably. The interior was dimmer than the lane. But that's only logical. He didn't think he was going to meet a ghost. Or a helpless maiden. He toyed with the idea of the sprawling maiden. But somehow didn't like it. The sprawling maidens he had read of and heard tell always appeared as if they were waiting for their cue. And this could be frightening. Really, he didn't think. The hind quarters of the building showed no signs of life. He had rather expected a bleary-eyed boy to be clanking and whacking and sousing saucers in the process called washing. But sometimes people just live in the front. And leave the back to the family ghosts. And never look back.

No one. And nothing. He went up the staircase he saw. At the top he could see a single window, paneless, in clear chiaroscuro to the surroundings. He went to it and looked out. He saw the court-yard, encased by two walls[4]. The sun could not get in directly. The view looked five-o'clockish.

He didn't walk through. He creaked the back door again to go home. Turning out of the lane he was momentarily awed by the brightness. It wasn't past one o'clock.

Sometimes, after doing his clever and neat homework, he went back. Sometimes, just for larks. It was always five o'clockish. Court-yard. Two walls. Sometimes when there was a breeze, he could see the little clinging plants vibrating. Once there were so many little plants that during a breeze, the walls did not look solid. He always enjoyed it.

But he didn't make a religion out of his OWN view. Which was why he enjoyed it.

HE WAS A young man when he met her; and she, though not exactly pretty, was quite presentable in their circle of friends. Neither of them was, in any sense, well-off. He was drawing a pretty meagre salary; and, as his wife, it was only expected that she had to make-do with the meagre salary. However, they were by no means poverty-stricken. They could, after some strenuous saving-exercises, afford such things as a little carpet-square for the bed-room, and the various ornaments, discreet in taste and quality, but displayed somewhat indiscreetly about. The better-off guests could discern some posturing in the wife when she affected to handle their few cut-glasses in a nonchalant fashion. The child they had, the only one, was quiet and highly manageable.

Then he made the great mistake of his life, incurring a big debt in one fierce gambling session.

It worried them a great deal, of course; and it sickened the wife for a good few days. But he took heart and began to figure out means to clear himself. At the salary he was drawing, together with his wife's paltry bit, it would take them some five years to annul the debt. But the debt, however, must be solvent at once. What could they do but do away with the few valuables they had, and the rest was a tug-of-war with the money-lenders. And then they found they were paying nothing but interest-money, while the original sum never seemed within their earthly power to equate.

The wife, after her early hysterics, accepted the fact in rather good taste; she began scouting for odd jobs. Soon she found that a few families were willing to have her to do their laundry, and to scrub the floors whenever the mistress of the house got into a hygienic fit. It was a back-breaking job, but she stuck to it. Which was both a reflection of her fortitude, and also her undoing. He, for his part (and a greater one), delivered papers before work, and at night he managed to find something at a printer's. It was a blind-alley job, supplementary though it was; all he had to do was to cut up stiffish paper into certain prescribed sizes, count to a hundred, then bind the lot with a strip of gummed paper. And he began to despair that the debt would ever be cleared within the five years he set. Then he would jerk down the cutting-blade with a sharper swish. She, too, felt the futility of the situation; perhaps more so, for in all fairness she should at least have been at the table and helped to roll the dice. After the first year, she let herself drift; she did not bother to keep house in the presentable way that she had done. And her own appearance could not be said to be over-neat. Her child was gone to her people, which of course caused a gulf between him and his parents. Finally, he sold himself, soul and all to his grandparents in return for loads of candy and a little affection. When he was a little older, in the period of sensitive youth, he felt a little ashamed of his parents when he did not see them; and the few times he did see them, he felt uneasy and rather alarmed. They could have been his uncle and aunt, so wide was the barrier now. One day, after visiting the child, the wife returned to her room and put away her little carpet-square. Though she neither had time nor the wish for idle probing of the heart, she felt that in some way she, as a woman, was insulted.

Ten years later and they were still insolvent; and the situation could hardly be said to have improved in another five years. By then, they were tired and the early enthusiasm of the first year seemed so much a thing of the past. Then the two people went about their work in a cheerless and mechanical manner. Work and pay, then more work and more work; then everything went to the pockets of those obnoxious and terrible money lenders. It was a stifling routine, for there was always a sense of the frantic, of rush and of ant-like industry. Sometimes, when the wife had a free hour to herself, she felt strange; something very familiar was amiss. But the years, like a few gulps of water, were swallowed and worried through; and whether the debt was clear or not; it wasn't very important.

A Silly Little Story 1964

WONG LOO WAS one of those persons who could not possibly have lived anywhere else except in Singapore. He was from China, speaking only the Cantonese dialect, but gradually he acquired a few words of English. Those few words he used in a well-meaning sort of way, but with some nonchalance as he was not very bothered about what they exactly meant. If one of his sons were to remark that a pop song which he had just heard was very witty, Wong Loo understood at once in his own way. He took it to mean that the song was silly, loud and noisy, and perhaps, in a plebeian sort of way, amusing. He could never, not even in one moment of soul-searching, have imagined that this debased son-of-a-pig could have found meaningfulness and significance in it. Therefore, Wong Loo was an ignorant man.

It could hardly be said that Wong Loo 'knew' Singapore. He was one of those people who could uproot himself to travel over a few thousand miles of ocean and when he reached, he promptly cast down all his roots again and adhered quietly but stoutly to his little area of animation. At this juncture, one may also have gathered that Wong Loo did not have a dynamic personality. But Wong Loo could not have wanted to live anywhere else now, except in Singapore. In an unreasonable frame of mind, he always thought Singapore was a no-man's land: his reasoning was most illogical—Singapore, a Malaysian state;[6] he himself, originally, a Chinese; every one speaks some English; and his unredeemable son hopped about to American pop songs. Sometimes, an odd French film is shown in one of those cinemas. But Wong Loo liked it all the same. As he very often pointed out, he had a basic approach to life; and his friends would say, yes, Wong Loo believes in tolerance. Wong Loo would nod in assent. His basic philosophy of life was: don't bother about things which you are not bothered with. For instance, sometimes he remembered that his grandmother used to tell him that the world was like one big, happy family. Wong Loo, of the unprogressive order, used to believe.

But now, in tranquillity,[7] he thought that his grandmother had been rather morbid.[8]

Wong Loo loved the Chinatown. He realized, of course, that the Chinatown of twenty years ago had more 'atmosphere'. But the die-hards were still around and he knew them, where to find them and for what he visits. He made a point to avoid the modernised shops, especially those that have plastic table-tops, plastic flowers and those infernal machines which jingle and jangle whenever a bill was paid. He loved the display of the sticky stalks of plum-flowers standing in big jugs of brine,[9] and which are available only at the New Year season.[10] He also enjoyed most of the articles on display in the shops—the odd items in furniture, the brass joss-stick containers, the miniature trees, the lacquer and the bamboo chop-sticks. His great favourite was an intricately carved Buddha, displayed on a shelf behind the counter and hidden by some brass-ware. He had once gone in to enquire about the price, and the owner of the shop, who wasn't Cantonese, managed to make him understand that it was made from a rare elephant's tusk and which had been a greatly admired object of one of the emperors, but it had been lost and was never heard of. Until now. In between lugging it out, slugging it on the counter and blowing at the dust, the shopkeeper asked for two thousand dollars.

For some weeks after, Wong Loo used to stop in front of the door, peer in and admired the Buddha. He wondered whether he should buy it. Finally he made up his mind. He wasn't going to care an elephant's flea about it anymore.

At home, Wong Loo always sat comfortably in his chair as he read the newspapers. He subscribed to the local Chinese newspapers and always read them all from page to page. He had no strong political beliefs. He disliked Communism for one reason only: that it has greatly disturbed Chinese traditions and turned the social order topsy-turvy. And so for this reason, besides other reasons, he liked Singapore. But also I think he could have been happy in, say, the Chinatown of San Francisco. Wong Loo was just plain and simply tolerant, and that was perhaps his saving grace. Therefore, a lot of things, big and small, did not irk him at all.

Soo Meng[11]

EVERY PERSON IN the neighbourhood knew that the Lims have three children. I am not sure why this was often mentioned in a manner that appeared to be like a verdict of some sort. Perhaps this was the problem: only two of the children are seen. Soo Eng and Soo Kong are often seen trotting alongside their mother on the way to the market and, like all other children who are too young to attend school, they are seen running about, in the field of the nearby church, running after the ice-cream man and mimicking his call, and generally running in and out of everyone's endurance. And where, or who, was the third child?

He's such a baby, so small, not strong, and the doctor has advised against exerting the child: Mrs. Lim's stock reply to any well-meaning person who would ask. But three months, half a year, one year ... was the child still such a tiny baby? not strong? Neighbours wondered and talked about it in between the intermittent conversations about their own children, recounting television programmes and topical subjects such as which diplomat has taken a holiday with which showgirl.[12] Why was the child concealed?

Could be a spastic case ... and I said to her, just between the two of us, why don't you take your baby out ... fresh air has never been known to kill anybody....

You shouldn't, that's crude. But I really wonder ... I remember saying to her once, no offence meant, my little boy's just beginning to crawl, so why don't you let him keep your baby company? For reasons of health, she says, but Ho! her other two kids tumble in and out of the house without so much as a sign of exhaustion.[13]

Last month, in the afternoon, a lorry ran over this child. At the time of this sad accident, Soo Meng, as was his name, was no longer a subject of speculation. The more kindly of the neighbours looked upon him instead as an object of pity. He was not, however, really such a baby anymore. He was slightly over five years old, a lovely child to look at and the slightly vacant look on his face made him different from many of the other children who are so quick to express their anger and happiness. Soo Meng was instead always even-tempered, even when being jostled about. He was born an idiot. And why not? It wasn't his choice (etc.), that much is obvious. The main thing was that he didn't look like one, not by a wide grin. He was liked by the other children and often police-and-thieved with them.

How this happened was simple enough. Nobody lives, really, in houses that have ten courtyards and fifty rooms. The Lims live in the kind of house that most people live in: the sort that one would move out of when, plonk, comes a windfall; the sort that the poor would be very glad to move into. Clearly then, Soo Meng could not be concealed for an eternity. One neighbour knew, must have known, and then all the neighbours. Now that this dark secret was out it was of no more interest to them. But Soo Meng could not, of course, be forgotten; not, at least, taken for granted as other children could be.

So Soo Meng had an ice-cream when Mrs. Ang bought ice-cream for her own kids. So he had some rambutans. So he had a wooden top. It was true that when Soo Meng looked at you like that, with a good-natured, slightly vacant look, how could any adult resist the strange impulse of not wanting to give him anything, the whole world—as an ice-cream cone? And also, how could the children prevent themselves from allowing him a bite off their cakes, to trot after them and to play with their toys?

That was it. I think it is one of those circumstances which would have proved harmless enough, and mundane, if things had gone a certain direction. For one thing, once a person knew that Soo Meng was an idiot, that was it. No one could possibly sustain surprise, pity or interest for a long time. But it could last a few months, a few years perhaps. Soo Meng was one of those unfortunates who would die either very young or very old. He could have lived to be a very old man cherishing himself with a vacant look. But it was not the way it happened. He was killed when he was five years old. At the time the neighbours 'discovered' him; he was already four years old. It was, then, one year of local, communal interest. Which, without the least intention on anyone's part, killed him.

But it is still that people are to blame. Especially now, when everyone seems to be in an emerging tempo. At one time, people might have laughed at an idiot; mothers might have plucked their children away from his breathing distance to leave him alone. I suppose people have now learnt not to let things be, without having to resort to tears, without sneers. One now surges forward to embrace a cause. Poor Soo Meng and, consequently, he gets a this, a that. It was a poor Soo Meng, all the more sad since he could never be any the wiser, who ran across the busy road to stop the Indian balloon-man. The one whom Mrs. Ang was calling out to.

Which balloon would Soo Meng have received?

The Effect of a Good Dinner

CUSTOM AND TRADITION are the easiest things to kill; even if they are not killed, they are easily jolted into a haemorrhage. Sometimes, they appear comical or ludicrous, or they are grim. When you cease to believe in them, you would seem to have come a long way. Sometimes, you may ask yourself: a long way from what? Then you may want to assert that, now, you do not have to tip-toe or kneel your way to where the angels and your ancestors were told to tread.[14]

This story is about my grand-uncle and my grand-aunt. They were not very loving. In fact, they did not seem to bother very much about each other and, in its way, it was a good thing. She was always busy with something: washing cups, babies, or stitching and sewing. He, too, was always busy; after all (he always said) a man has to work to keep his family very fully alive. By this, it is meant that a person sometimes has to buy his eldest son a bicycle, his eldest daughter a portable radio (to sew by), his wife a jade bangle, and himself a car. Seen in a coolly detached manner, my grand-uncle's family was not very interesting: every now and again, someone failed or passed an examination, one of the younger children fell off the bicycle, the battery went flat in the radio. Life was complacent and there was neither domestic tragedy nor sublimation. They carried on without having to insert coins into slot-machines or, on the other hand, to labour in the fields.

Year by year, something gives and fizzles out. New Year doesn't come half as exciting as did the previous. The Moon Festival[15] seems more insipid. The children no longer bother to rise very early to bathe and put on their new clothes.[16] Besides such little things, the custom of marriage, in my grand-uncle's household at least, had also changed. Marriage in those days was by the process of match-making. There were, and are, a horde of such professional match-makers who set themselves into everybody's confidence and, finally, help these people to sort out their sons and daughters for marriage. The two persons to be married need not know each other, but after a quietly nervous meeting, they should. This aspect of marriage becomes less and less comprehensible to people today. Match-making has nothing much to commend it. Though divorces are never heard of, this does not lend evidence to the belief that these married people are happy and contented. More often than not, the husbands 'acquire' new wives. My grand-uncle's children do not count in this. They were not, or were not going to be, match-made. If there was an ugly girl or an idiotic boy in the family, then things might have been slightly different. But usually, by a family's own standards, there are simply no such things. So the people who have any interest for me are my grand-uncle and my grand-aunt.

It is never unfashionable for a person to have a concubine. Also, it is never the policy for the wife to forbid her husband this little whim as long as he doesn't squeeze her allowance to rice-powder. My grand-uncle certainly had the means and my grand-aunt the understanding. In most cases, a wife accepted it as a matter of course. Her only misgiving might be that she might not feel amiable towards the new wife but, in such a case, it would only be a slight misgiving on her part. The greater and silent misgiving would be that the new wife might not be amiably disposed towards her, and what with her fresher appeal, her comparative youth and his new allegiance, the woman usually stood in mortal dread of a domestic turmoil. Her consolation would be that life itself, like some table game, would still have built-in surprises.

Their background is uncomplicated.[17] They came over from China at a very early age with their parents. My grand-aunt stayed in the house at all times and grew up; my grand-uncle attended the early part of school and also grew up. One day, they were married. The match-maker received the customary "red-packet",[18] eggs dyed a red colour,[19] roast pork and, depending on her persuasiveness, many other things. Gradually, they prospered. They had many children. My grand-uncle began to wear shirts in place of singlets, or Mandarin coats for social functions; my grand-aunt had her hair waved and wore it that way till she was much older. They acquired new habits and gave over their old ones. But still they did not give away everything. There wasn't any need to. In their heyday, Singapore wasn't so instant. And when they had passed their heyday, they were not so ready to be influenced, or to change their ways. The change in the children was considerably greater, and it was all a part of a social process, called inevitably, the process of growing up.

The war also came, but it did not last forever. Then a few more years and only those who were in it remembered and recounted its aspects. But the war also brought with it a sudden lull and a disenchanted attitude in people. When the better years came, there was a quickening of merriment and, when this came, it came doubly quick and appeared to be quite contagious. The result of it all, in my grand-uncle's pacifistic household, was that he wanted my grand-aunt's cousin, a comparatively young woman, as the second wife.[20] This was part of the quickening process. During the war, they did not suffer unduly. (They had friends who did.) Things had been generally scarce. It was now time, and not too late surely, to make compensations. After all, during the war one had to make sacrifices.[21] Society, of course, had to. During peace-time, it regained its feet— shrugged off its empty and demented buildings, and, step by step, it repaired, improved and modified itself. But there were certain things that society could not provide. We like to think so, sometimes. My grand-uncle thought so and, as always, he did not directly relate such thoughts to himself. Always, there was some person enacting the victim for him. To my grand-uncle, society could not provide the happiness of that person sitting in that rattan arm-chair and looking out into that pokey little garden. Then, boom: society could now give him a plush arm-chair, an obedient garden. But they are not the same, he cried. They are not. My uncle was not the same.

What could my grand-uncle have wanted? Perhaps if there had been no war he would not have wanted anything, much. But there was the war. He did not start it. He did not end it. It was there. And now that it was over, he could forget it and again lead a more organized life.

If everyone had agreed to what he wanted, there would have been a feast, and the first wife would have had a cup of tea served her by the new.[22] And the new wife would have, in turn, received one of those three unlegislated things: a poisonous glare, a look of relief, a look of total resignation. But she did not receive any of these things. My grand-aunt did not have her tea.

After my grand-uncle had announced his intention, my grand-aunt went quietly to her mother (who was still fiercely alive) and also to her closer relatives and friends. In place of a feast, there was a scene—not a scene in the sense of a "show-down", but in the sense that these people made something happen at a particular place, at a particular time. (Now, if you were one of the detached servants, or a bird perching outside the window, you could also have seen it.)

My grand-aunt's supporters then went to see my grand-uncle. He was kind and entertained their opinions. They did not want him to marry the wife's cousin. It wasn't that my grand-aunt was jealous. Really, she wasn't. Nor was it solely because she was afraid that the new wife might usurp her. Nor was bigamy considered wrong or something to be ashamed of. Right, wrong, shame are the moral goodies one tumbles out of one's bag when there is nothing else. This was what my grand-aunt believed.

My grand-aunt's dislike for her cousin was not merely personal. The personal element, of course, did come in. But more than that, their two families, though closely related, had never been cordial or kindly disposed towards each other. After the initial stage of disagreement, all the novelty of dislike and petty feuding was gone. In its place, a more restrained, but more bitter, attitude had set in. Quarrels were no longer so noisy nor so enthusiastically participated in, but the words were more stinging and more sincerely expressed. It would be a great loss of face then if my grand-uncle were to marry his wife's cousin. My grand-aunt's mother and relatives and friends had therefore gathered that day to bring a petition. As on all such occasions, there was a promise of drama. But every now and again, this was marred when someone sobbed too unashamedly, or did not quite come in on cue. My grand-aunt was more dignified and remained quite impassive about it all. The important thing was that they wanted to find out exactly how great was my grand-uncle's need of a second wife and, in particular, of this woman. Finally, it was known that another wife, be she cousin or no cousin, was in dire need.

Then dinner was announced. The presence of a big spread of food always makes people stop being serious. The relatives and friends heartily ate up their well-deserved meal. One great thing about a good meal is that, besides satisfying hunger, it usually has a very calming effect on a person's ruffled feelings and also a soothing effect on his internal emotional flap.

After the dinner, the old man was presented with the decision that he should not pursue any further his desire to marry the cousin, but that he could have, as second wife, any other decent woman he should choose.

None the Wiser

MEI CHING WENT towards the window and pushed the glasspanes back. She stretched out her arm to find the catch. Teng Soo, sitting behind her, thought for one amusing moment that his wife was extending her arms into the sky to help the weather.

Rain was pouring down.

The open window made the room cooler. Later on, in the evening, they would be attending a birthday dinner. It ought to be grand enough. It was in honour of Mei Ching's mother. Ever since Teng Soo could remember, his wife's mother had always been so aged-looking. She had brought up her own children and, now, their children. Everything had turned out well and, in particular for Kok Lian, Mei Ching's brother, who had become the director of Lucky Advertising. Later on, then, they would be going to his house where the dinner was to be.

Sitting under the ornate ceiling-lamp, Mei Ching winked unobtrusively at Teng Soo. She added a quick upward tilt of her nose. Teng Soo smiled at the pretence of the chandelier-like lamp. It was garishly fashioned. It must also be costly. Teng Soo was averse to anything that hinted of wealth, particularly of waste. He was bored with his work as an insurance clerk. Whenever utterly bored, he interested himself in the background details of his clients. Mei Ching taught at the Sunrise Kindergarten, a private and exclusive concern, exclusive because very few parents could afford to send their children to a private kindergarten.

"May you live a long life".
"Happiness and prosperity".

These were some of the warm wishes offered to old Mrs Tan. She sat contentedly in the blue vinyl armchair, nodded her head appreciatively. After each greeting, she would mutter the name of the well-wisher, almost as some kind of assurance that age has its own litany.

"Mei Ching, Teng Soo".

"Kok Beng".

And, also, an indifferent "Fee Li" to her daughter-in-law. Outside, at the doorway, was hung the customary red sash.[23]

For Kok Lian, the occasion was a gathering of the family. For the others, it was a time to have dinner and a merry, noisy evening. Old Mrs Tan has been living with Kok Lian ever since her other children started work and eventually moved out of the terrace-house they were living in at one time. Mei Ching, her only daughter, and Teng Soo live in one of the Queenstown flats.[24] Of her two other children, Kok Beng studied chemical engineering at the Sydney University. After completing his course, he returned with his degree and his Australian wife. They live in one of the new flats built quite close to the Katong Park.[25] The conservative Mrs Tan still has an almost instinctive timidity as well as dislike of Phyllis. At times, she is too kind, too generous towards Phyllis. On other occasions, she is totally indifferent and cold. But having lived through the winters in Australia, Phyllis is never unduly disturbed by this discrepancy.[26]

"Are you feeling better these days?" Phyllis asked Li May, Kok Lian's wife.

"Yes, thank you. But I get tired so easily."

Li May has been ill recently and was still looking it. When Mei Ching and Kok Beng moved away to live on their own, Kok Lian did so as well. He bought the house that he and Li May now live in. They gave up the lease of the terrace-house. Mrs Tan came with them. For her, it was simply a transfer of locality. Kok Lian is her eldest child. Moreover, she helps to look after the grandchildren. Each year sees her even more harassed while the grandchildren grow from strength to strength.

After dinner, Mrs Tan got up. Lately, she smiled much more and also seemed more easily flustered.

"I am going upstairs."

She waved her hands awkwardly, as if every action of hers was a liability.

"No, it's quite all right. Don't worry about me. You young people have so much energy and so many things to talk about."

"I'll go up with you, mother," Mei Ching offered.

"Don't worry about me, Ching. Sit down and chat with the others. It is so seldom that I can have you all here together."

"I'll see you upstairs, ma." Li May got up. "I'm going up as well. The silly pills the doctor gave me make me feel so sleepy."

"Yes, you run along to bed," said Kok Lian.

"Yes. I'll see ma to her room first. Goodnight."

"Goodnight."

"Have a good rest. Mother. May."

"Sleep well."

Kok Lian watched his mother walk slowly up the staircase. One hand was feeling the wall. With the other, she was holding on to Li May. Pausing for a moment, she called out, "Don't forget to pull the sash back, Lian. I forgot to tell you earlier. It is raining and I don't want the dye to drip on the floor."

"All right, ma."

Kok Lian was silent for a few minutes. No wonder May is so weak. She has never been in good health, and looking after the old woman certainly does not improve it. Now that the old woman has gone to bed, Kok Lian broached the subject—that either Mei Ching or Kok Beng should 'take over' their mother.

"How can we?" Teng Soo sounded angry. "Mei Ching works as well. Who's going to look after her during the day? The cat?"

"Anyway, our cubicle[27] is too small even for us," added Mei Ching.

She felt a little uneasy about refusing, as one would initially feel when refusing to give help of any kind. But she had reason and was searching for a sounder one. She wanted a reason sounder to herself. It was difficult to instance any. She shook her head in anger. As she did so, she caught sight of the garishly-fashioned lamp and suddenly felt that she hated it.

"I would love to have mother with us," Kok Beng said, "but I don't think she'll take to Phyllis's cooking."

"It's perfectly all right. Mother can cook." Mei Ching was quick to point this out.

"Yes, she cooks well too. You see, I'm not trying to push her on to you all. But May is in such poor health and ...."

Here, Kok Lian was interrupted by Teng Soo.

"She shouldn't be really. Unless, of course, May does all the work and leaves your amah in total ease. Actually, the question is not whether mother should live with us," and nodding to Kok Beng, "or you."

"You mean she's to live alone? Or perhaps you'd lend her your cat?" Kok Beng said curtly.

"No. There's no need to. Well, you see, mother can go and live with somebody. Or in some institution. But we have to agree on how to settle the expenditure."

"You mean—gosh! You mean we should send mother to the Home for the Aged?"[28] Kok Beng became heated.

"How can you think of an idea like that! It's awful!"

Phyllis looked a little shocked, a little fascinated.

Mei Ching, who had been silent for a while, began to offer reasons for her husband's suggestion.

"It's not a bad idea really. Not if you think in terms of something practical. Mother isn't going to enjoy herself if she comes to us. It isn't as if we are having a whale of a time either."

"But a Home! Well, if it's for the best, then I mean ... Gosh! It's still awful." Phyllis still looked a little shocked, a little fascinated.

There was a sudden silence. The regular and monotonous

pattering of the rain could be heard. Kok Lian got up and went to pull back the flap-ends of the sash. But the sash was already wet. As he lifted one of the flaps, he could feel the heaviness of the soaked fabric. The dye ran faintly in his palm. He let the flap go, without any more concern.

"No, I won't let mother go to the Home."

All eyes turned to Kok Lian. After all, he was the one who started all the fuss. This damn fool wants to be the filial son, thought Teng Soo scornfully. For one amusing moment, he had the idea that Kok Lian was going to rip off the sash, girt it round his waist and brandish a sword in defiance of the Home.

Mrs Tan did not go to the Home. The morning after her celebration she reminisced over the occasion. She was none the wiser.

"Did you ask Beng to give Mei Ching and Teng Soo a lift? I hope they didn't leave too early. It's so seldom that you all meet together."

The Story of a Mask[29]

CHINESE OPERA HAD, of course, its origin in China. Its progression and fruition were also in China, but waves of this particular operatic influence radiated outwards and hung up its curtains in other countries. Occasionally, a few actors who were not eking out an adequate living, decided to come to the Nanyang[30] (Malaya and Singapore) and start afresh.

The less successful ones led rather dreary lives, but that was many years ago in China, before the Cultural Revolution.[31] There, they played to wealthy noblemen who, because they were wealthy, paid them little attention or money. They played at the roadside, to scurrying men with bags of rice or firewood for delivery and who only paused to watch, to children, to housewives shopping for their daily requirements; all to whom, because they were poor, gave them nothing. But the process went on, the troupes existing on meagre fare. They slept below the make-shift stages wherever they were, on long narrow benches which were uncomfortable and did nothing to help them. Their profession was a difficult one but they had not savoured enough ease to want to strive for a life of comfort.

Those who came to Singapore found that their lives were essentially the same. Perhaps this was because they could not yet afford to be ambitious. They still played on make-shift stages in the streets and they still made the best of an existence from the coins collected at the end of each performance. This, they told everyone. They brought with them, among other things, their beliefs, their superstitions and folkways and, when they were unhurried (which was quite often), they looked around and saw that, though they felt unchanged, they were in fact changed. Change was inevitable and it was inevitable also for opera actors. They found that these changes had become very much a part of their lives, and it was by recounting the things of the past that they were able to trace the differences between themselves then and themselves now.

Singapore prospered. And with greater purchasing ability people could now afford some culture. The rich gave their relatives prints of birds and mountains. Opera, given a kick, reared to its heyday. Permanent theatres were set up, notably the ones in the Great World, the New World and the Happy World.[32] These Worlds, too, had changed.

They were then rambling places where food-stalls were huddled in a corner, two cinemas in another, a carousel and a "ghost train" in the centre, the theatre in another corner. And visitors filled up the remaining space in the evening.

One troupe, in particular, felt the new lifestyle all the more because it had always been the poorest. The members of this troupe were accustomed to being pathetically poor. The actors had to save part of their ration of uncooked rice and pound it into a fine powder. This, mixed with water, would be applied on their faces before they went to stage. One actor, in particular, had dire need of it; he played, unfailingly, the role of the hero. His whole face, on stage, was white, save for very black eyebrows and very carmine lips. To look through his symbolic value and discern the real person would have been a difficult task. One could see only the deadpan look, of a mask. Even though life in the troupe was now more comfortable, this actor's face was still the same whitened object. On stage, he was totally impersonal. It did not bother the members of the audience unduly as they were accustomed to the clear-cut distinction between good and evil. Invariably, they loved him. Their sympathies were for him. They quivered in anger when the villain placed obstacles in his path, they glowed with good cheer when he triumphed over the villain in the end. Yet, were they to meet him in the street, they would have just walked past him without a second glance. Wong Loo was that nondescript.

The good times did not last. The interest in Chinese wayang,[33] as it is called, was spasmodic and short-lived. Though in its short span of popularity much had been done by way of setting up permanent theatres with steady and apparently unflinching patronage, yet when the interest waned, the theatres were easily adapted as showrooms for Chinese medicine or fabrics. The staunch patrons now ran their fingers over the fine linens or sought advice from the girls at the counter regarding cures for headaches, heartburn and a host of other little illnesses.

Wong Loo and his troupe were now forced back to their former poverty-stricken way of life. Wong Loo had, by this time, become one of those who could not possibly live anywhere else except in Singapore. He had uprooted himself from China and travelled over a few thousand miles of ocean. When he reached Singapore, he had promptly cast down all his roots again and adhered quietly but firmly to his little area of animation. Certain customs and superstitious beliefs still persisted. He still believed that each night, when a person is sleeping, the soul departs from the body to return again when dawn arrives.[34] It was that element of fascination in such a belief that awed him and he was convinced, unquestioningly, by that fascination. But he began to lose his faith in other beliefs. He remembered that his grandmother used to tell him that the world was like one big, happy family. Wong Loo, then of the unprogressive order, used to believe it. But now, in tranquillity, he thought that his grandmother had been rather morbid.[35]

Wong Loo still slept on one of the long, narrow benches. Each night, he believed that as he slept, his tired soul left him to wander apace. Each morning, it returned. For some reason, which he could not explain, he felt a little cheered. Accordingly, he set about tending to whatever job he had. As he and the troupe were no longer engaged for frequent performances, they had the time and the need to take on little extra jobs, the making of paper lanterns, of fragrant joss-sticks, of wooden containers for holding the joss-sticks. As far as performances were concerned, they were now relying on festive occasions, such as the Moon Festival or the New Year, to provide them with employment. These are the occasions which demand a festive atmosphere and wayang supplied the necessary pomp and colour.

Chinatown was ablaze with colour. It was the New Year season. Wong Loo's troupe was hired to give three performances, the second and major performance to fall on the eve of the New Year. The performances were to be acted on a make-shift stage, erected in one of the streets. Wong Loo felt that warm feeling again rekindling itself in him. He loved the display of the sticky stalks of plum flowers standing in big jugs of brine which are available only during this time. He also enjoyed most of the articles on display in the crowded shops — the odd items of furniture, the joss-stick containers (some of which he had made), the miniature trees, the lacquer, the bamboo containers.[36] Fire-crackers exploded freely. Children scurried about with bulging pockets of sweets and tangerines. Chinatown, in short, seemed determined to put forward its very best front. The other days of the year did not seem to matter much, only the few days of the New Year season seemed important, and as a result, there was a big surge of merriment. To Wong Loo, those few days seemed frantically real. He was determined to make the second performance a truly memorable one.

He had spent many days cleaning his stage costumes and had helped to repair whatever damage had been done to their stage properties. The days were spent in happy anticipation of that particular performance. With the money given him before the performance to enable him to take part in the festivities he acquired some new clothes and also pooled his money with the others in the troupe so that they would be able to have a grand dinner before the main performance.

On New Year's Eve, Wong Loo and his fellow-actors did not retire till about one o'clock in the morning. They had been giving their performance and, before that, there had been the dinner. Wong Loo enjoyed himself, his companions were toasting and jabbering away with much mirth. On stage, they had gone through the whole gamut of quiet symbolic emotions. But the drums were ear-shattering, the audience rowdy. Wong Loo had spent considerable time, after dinner, in putting on his stage clothes and in painting his face an even, unflinching white except for the carmine lips and the very black eyebrows. Everyone enjoyed the performance. The enjoyment was due partly to the enthusiasm of the season. Also, the audience felt free enough to wander around the streets, only to come back later for snatches of the performance. The actors felt freer too and felt much less obliged to put on a good act. Consequently, the performance was better and the audience, in turn, received it well.

After the performance, everyone was tired; the hero extremely so. He laid himself on the bench without having removed his mask. His soul, as usual, left to wander. In the early hours, with the slow intrusion of light, it flittered back and hung quiveringly over the bench, and then retreated.[37] The limp body was not familiar: it was slumped on the bench, but its face was not as usual. It was still and white, a mockery of the real thing.

Next morning, they found him dead.

A Beginning and a Middle
Without an Ending[38]   1982, rev. 1993

WHEN IT GOT to about ten o'clock, the incessant chatter started to peter off.[39] Leng Eng turned to Elaine and asked if her sister would sing a song. Even in asking, Leng Eng was not herself convinced that it was a good idea. It was a dull gathering, a gaggle of girls who, like herself, had completed school a few years back.[40] Similarly, if Jimmy had been free, why would she, Leng Eng, be with them?

Hurry up! Elaine's tone, while not as sharp as when rapping out orders at home, was commanding enough. Betty got up and walked to the centre of the room. She showed no awkwardness or embarrassment at being thus singled out. At twelve, she showed a resilience beyond her years. There was something rather vacuous about her face.

What's going on?

My sister's going to sing a song. You don't mind?

What's there to mind? Sing what?[41]

Betty started singing a song in Mandarin.[42] She had heard that song often enough to have learnt it by rote.[43] When she first heard it performed by a Taiwanese singer, she there and then decided it would be a song she would sing forever. That Taiwanese singer had been sensational. At every performance, she ended the song with tears hosing down her face. To Betty, it was not only moving; it was like having access to an entire vista of human understanding that had so far eluded her.

Her earnest strong voice and impassive face struck the audience[44] as comic. But she sang in obedience to the mannerly deployment of her heart. Her voice soared and, when she came to the end and had hit the last note, she fell onto the floor in a heap.

Bring a towel. Quick![45] Leng Eng screamed, more in anger than concern.[46]

Elaine, bent over her sister, suddenly straightened herself. Betty stood up. And Elaine, who had heard her practising the song so often quickly understood what it was all about.[47] Betty had wanted to extend the Taiwanese singer's presentation.[48] In place of tears, Betty had chosen the faint, the dramatic crumble. A sense of admiration, shame and anger welled up; Elaine got up and gave Betty a resounding slap.[49]

The dull gathering ended on a merry note for nearly everyone. And Betty—who could tell what she felt? Leng Eng started praising Betty; the suppressed snigger and muffled laughter around her was ambient support.[50]

You must come more often. Can't hide all that talent, you know.[51] Elaine, you must enter her[52] for the talentime.[53] Whether she wins or not, sure to floor the judges.

Leng Eng was stacking glasses and plates on a tray.[54]

Want some more coffee or not? Better say so,[55] if not no time to make some more.[56]

———

Later, thirty-five years later, Betty was the executive director of a modelling school.

Excuse me, Miss Wong, got two more enrolled this morning. Want to accept or not?[57]

The new secretary did not last long.

You have to speak correctly.[58] Above everything else, you must have poise. In speaking[59] to you, the participants, the photographers, whoever they are, must feel as if you are confiding in them. Betty Wong, in her advice to the secretary being interviewed, was herself confident[60] and highly poised. Her string of pearls secreted the wisdom of the sea. There is so much unhappiness in the world.[61] If I could educate every Woman to be elegant and charming, half the troubles of the world would be gone. You must understand, such education is the most difficult to instil in people. We have to work very hard. We have to make sacrifices.[62]

Betty Wong levitated from her chair and, in crossing the room in regular, heart-felt steps, thought fleetingly of a song she could no longer fully remember.

Oh, hello, Vicki,[63] Your show was fantastic! Such classical lines! Such poetry of motion![64]

Vicki held on[65] the elegant white telephone, her hand a nubile technological extension. Oh, right, right! It doesn't matter. I'll call again. Hey Betty, you know what?[66] Benny's going to have a show[67] in Manila next month.

Who's financing it? I see, I see, and all expenses paid for. What! Twenty-five percent guaranteed sales.[68]

Betty Wong inclined her head a little and both her hands described quarter-circles of beatitude. It isn't so much the financial success. Just imagine what Benny can and must do. What an educational experience it will have to be.[69]

Betty returned to her office. In the eggshell splendour, a secondary thought raced through her mind. I must send Elaine some money. She is, after all, my sister. Should I send her a thousand? She wrote out a cheque for two hundred, lit a cigarette, buzzed the intercom, tore up the cheque and, when the new secretary came in, she was frowning over a letter like an octopus that had organized its tentacles over a sheet of seaweed. She did not look up immediately; and when she did,[70] the secretary's obedient eyes immediately[71] rolled away. Betty Wong smiled an interior smile, a little mental[72] zip had been pulled. An old trick, she thought, but how effective. The secretary was very brand new.[73]

It wasn't Cent meditation I dictated. It was Zen meditation.[74] Z for Zip. You have been very remiss.

re: Miss Zatika
I regret to inform you that the nominee you
proposed for our course on Inner Poise and
Cent Meditation has been unsuccessful.

Miss Zatika, prior to nomination, had been Au Lin Soo, a healthy fresh-face. Why would spring lamb want to pass off as meditative mutton?[75] Such a thought was not in Betty Wong's ideational agenda.[76]

But if she likes, she could try again.[77]

Her letter to the director of a lesser-known modelling school was one she had sent off hundreds of times. The difference each time was that the name was different. The name of the course was also different. Last week, she regretted the rejection[78] of a participant for The Externalization Of[79] Inner Light.

Betty Wong felt tired. All these trivial details. There is absolutely no one one can depend on. She had wanted, every single day, to plan and map out her Beauty Edification Project. A nearby file carried the inscription:

DhPP/II/16A
Physiognometrics—Within and[80] Without
Beauty, the Art and the Science of, and the
Philosophy of[81]

Apart from the inscription, the file was empty, without.

———

An ending must be found. Without it, Betty Wong could only go on rejecting the Zatikas. The Zatikas are abundant. Somewhere in between the rejection and the realization that the Zatikas were being rejected for nothing, for things that weren't there; somehow, in between the chuckle and the choke, Betty Wong drew a conclusion. It was the collapse before the song started. And poor Elaine, the face, the recollection of the face that could not launch Betty Wong's hand.[82]

Notes

[1] The Yap family employed an *amah* to look after the infant Arthur Yap during the 1940s at their residence in Kim Seng Road.

[2] *Mandore*: not found in OED, but apparently means "road mender". *See* "Mandore Jailed for Theft", *Singapore Free Press*, 24 December 1947, p. 5.

[3] Singapore Anti Tuberculosis Association, an expatriate voluntary organization that began in 1947.

[4] Yaps description of a shop-house with a "court-yard encased by two walls", which the protagonist views from an upstairs window, appears to correspond to a style of shop house featuring a rear courtyard. However, the description of a dim interior when entering from the back street door may suggest rather an absence of a rear courtyard. In this case, the schoolboy could be viewing from the upstairs window not a rear courtyard, but perhaps an airwell. *See* "Variations of Shop-house", Singapore Urban Redevelopment Authority Conservation Guidelines, December 2011.

[5] An allusion to the first and second Malayan 5-year Plan (1956–65), which has its origin in the Russian soviet model. It was later deployed as a title for Singaporean public housing policies.

[6] From September 1963 to August 1965, Singapore was a member of the Federation of Malaysia.

[7] William Wordsworth defined poetry as "the spontaneous overflow of powerful emotions recollected in tranquillity", "Preface" to *Lyrical Ballads*.

[8] The preceding two sentences are recycled and reworked in "The Story of a Mask".

[9] Plum blossoms are traditionally used as decoration during the Chinese New Year.

[10] Occurring in late January to early February, the longest and most important festivity in the Chinese calendar.

[11] One of Yap's neighbours at River Valley Road was an endearing mentally handicapped child.

[12] Singapore Television broadcasts began in 1963. In June 1966, Singapore's former second Chief Minister and later Malaysian High Commissioner to Australia, 51-year-old Lim Yew Hock disappeared for ten days. He was subsequently discovered, after a much publicized search in Australia. The press subsequently reported on his association with 19-year-old Sydney stripper Sandra Nelson.

[13] Here perhaps, we encounter Yap's first sustained representation of local speech patterns. Rather than the democratized Singlish/patois suggested in "two mothers in a hdb playground" (1980), here ten years earlier, we encounter the standard, studied, English of an upper middle class urban Singaporean neighbourhood of the 1960s. The expression "without so much as a sign of exhaustion" is reminiscent of curious constructions of good Chinese Singaporean English.

[14] An allusion to Alexander Pope's "For fools rush in where angels fear to tread", *An Essay on Criticism* (1711).

[15] Chinese Mid-Autumn (harvest festival), occurring in September–October.

[16] The passing away of this minor ritual in Singapore about the mid-1960s was an indirect effect of Westernization, modernization and perhaps redevelopment.

[17] Bearing in mind Singapore's immigrant past, the narrator's description of grand-uncle and grand-aunt's background as "uncomplicated" (28) seems disingenuous.

[18] A monetary gift given on special occasions.

[19] In Chinese tradition, red is the colour of prosperity.

[20] In 1961, the passage of the Women's Charter put polygamy to an end. However, even prior to that, it was only practiced by the wealthy elite among Chinese Singaporeans.

[21] The phrase is also used in a more nuanced sense in Yap's last short story, "A Beginning and a Middle without an Ending", which features an imagined representation of twenty-first century, Singapore.

[22] In the case of marriage to a second wife, the first wife, along with other relatives of the groom, would be served tea by the new wife at a traditional Chinese tea ceremony.

[23] A festive red banner sash is traditionally hung over the front door to ward off evil.

[24] This is the sole reference in Yap's short stories to government housing. Queenstown, a Singapore Improvement Trust public housing estate in Singapore begun in 1953. Mei Ching's name echoes that of a section of the estate, Mei Chin (meaning beautiful view" in Mandarin").

[25] Katong Park is not far from Marine Parade where the Yap family relocated from River Valley Road in the 1970s. It was a popular Singaporean public space from the 1930s to the 1960s. A decade or so later, the time in which the action of "None the Wiser" is set, the recent redevelopment of the East Coast had left the park landlocked, reduced and neglected though still a comparatively desirable location to live in Singapore, c. 1965–75.

[26] One might recall Teng Soo's association of Mrs Tan's daughter Mei Ching with the weather at the beginning of the story.

[27] In Singaporean parlance of the period, "cubicle" indicates in this context an HDB one-room flat, housing of the most rudimentary and basic variety, principally built for low-income families.

[28] The issue of "the Home for the Aged" highlights a topical dialogue between traditional and modern Singaporean points of view in which filial piety contests with expedience and practicality.

[29] The National Library of Singapore has a recording of Yap reading this story in 1985.

[30] Nanyang: "Southern Ocean". "The [historical] Chinese name for: South-East Asia; the seas around this region" (OED).

[31] Cultural Revolution: a reform movement in communist China, begun in 1966, whose aim was to combat revisionism by restoring pure Maoist doctrine.

[32] The Great World, the New World and the Happy World: amusement parks opened by Chinese businessmen in the 1920–30s. In these spaces, Singaporeans of all classes mingled freely. The Great World was within walking distance of Yap's childhood home in River Valley Road. The Happy World was in Geylang and the New World in Serangoon Road. Cantonese and Malay opera were also very popular in Singapore during the prosperous late colonial period 1930–65. In the "Worlds", Chinese opera competed with other, newer, amusements, such as *gewutuan*, a variety show originating in China, "taxi-girls" who could be hired for dances, as well as fair rides, theatrical revues, and cinema.

[33] By the time Yap wrote this story, the term *wayang* referred almost exclusively to Chinese opera.

[34] The belief in the soul leaving the body at night is a traditional Chinese belief. According to Chinese legend, a human being has two souls: a superior, spiritual soul (*hun*) and an inferior, material soul (*p'o*). As a person sleeps, the superior soul can wander while the inferior soul stays with the body If the superior soul becomes detached from the body through death the soul wanders the world till it finds a body it wants to enter. Some traditions believe this will only happen to the spiritually conscious such as shamen or to the physically sick. In this state the person can commune with other worlds and other spirits. It is interesting that Wong Loo seems reinvigorated/ cheered on waking ("Each morning it returned. For some reason which he could not explain, he felt a little cheered."), suggesting the benefits of this momentary spiritual-metaphysical escape from the restrictions of a material Singapore. Chinese Singaporean children in pre-independence Singapore were admonished not to put make-up on a sleeping person lest the soul was unable to recognise the body and fail to return thereto.

[35] This sentence is reworked from "A Silly Little Story".

[36] This sentence is reworked from "A Silly Little Story".

[37] A seemingly familiar word but in fact another curious use by Yap of an English archaism—meaning "flitting about, fluttering, trembling, shifting, unstable, fleeting" (OED). As a former St Andrew's schoolboy and a literature graduate at the University of Singapore, Yap may have been aware of John Milton's use of the word in the MS draft of *Comus* (1634). Yap's deployment of the archaism also suggests that Wong Loo's belief is also old, perhaps outmoded, and increasingly difficult to access from a modern Singaporean perspective.

[38] This story was first published in *Tenggara*, Vol. 11 (1982), 17–20. A revised version appeared in *S. E. Asia Writes Back; Skoob Pacific Anthology, No. 1* (London: Skoob Books, 1993), 75–8. The later, revised version of the story has been anthologized in *People on the Bridge; An Anthology of ASEAN Short Stories*, ed. Amilah Ab. Rahman and Nor Azmah Shehidan (Dewan Bahasa dan Pustaka, 2001). More recently, the story has appeared in *One. The Anthology*, ed. Robert Yeo (Singapore: Marshall Cavendish, 2012). The 1993 revisions, while minor, are in my opinion telling enhancements. Thus it is the 1993 text that I reprint here. I supply the significant variant readings below.

[39] Yap's narrator as well as his characters in this story appears to deploy a studiedly, subtly inaccurate form of standard English.

[40] The 1982 version includes at this point: "The met infrequently here and never brought along their boyfriends." The addition of this sentence means the following sentence makes more sense.

[41] "Sing what?" A Singlish phrase meaning: "why not? Go on, sing."

[42] The Speak Mandarin campaign was launched by Lee Kuan Yew in 1979; other Chinese dialects were actively discouraged. The increasing prominence of Mandarin in Singapore from 1979 indicates something of a volte face a decade or so after the PAP leader's original policy of promoting English as a democratizing lingua franca for Chinese, Malays, Indians, and Eurasians in Singapore.

[43] 1982: "learnt it".

[44] 1982: "listeners".

[45] 1982: insert "Also some water."

[46] 1982: "more in anger." The 1993 version gestures to a parody and a reworking of Horatio's description of the facial expression of the ghost of Hamlet's father as a "countenance more in sorrow than in anger" (1. 2. 231).

[47] 1982: "was about."

[48] 1982: "Taiwanese's presentation."

[49] 1982: "and slapped Betty."

[50] 1982: paragraph continues.

[51] 1982: "talent you know."

[52] 1982: "Elaine, must enter her".

[53] A local talent show televised on Radio Television Singapore confirms the temporal setting of this section of the story as the late 1960s to the mid-1970s.

[54] 1982: paragraph continues.

[55] 1982: "Better say so quickly."

[56] 1982: "make some more later."

[57] The connotations of Yap's often subtle deployment of authentic Singlish in this story is something that a Malaysian readership are likely to have been attuned to on its first publication in *Tenggara* in 1982. However, a more international audience are likely to have missed those connotations when the story was republished in the UK in 1993.

[58] Betty's pronouncement seems a gentle satire on 1980s anxieties, reflecting and foreshadowing Singapore's Speak Good English Movement that started in 2000.

[59] 1982: "talking".

[60] 1982: "confidential".

[61] 1982: "troubles world".

[62] The phrase seems to tellingly echo early Singaporean government rhetoric.

[63] 1982: "Vick!"

[64] Ironically Betty gets the phrase wrong. While at St Andrews, Yap had published in the 1962 school annual a poem titled "Poetry in Motion".

[65] 1982: "reached for".

[66] 1982: "do you know what?"

[67] 1982: "organizing a show"

68 1982: paragraph continues.

69 1982: "it must be."

70 1982: "when she abruptly did,"

71 1982: "suddenly".

72 1982: "inner".

73 Yap again plays on bad "good English".

74 1982: "It was Zen".

75 A curious reversal of the phrase "mutton dressed as lamb". The phrase "meditative mutton" appears in Ambrose Bierce, *The Fables of Zambri, the Parsee* (1872–3).

76 It is unclear if in referring to Betty's "ideational agenda" Yap is referring to the original nineteenth century meaning of "ideational" ("Of or pertaining to ideation or the formation of ideas."), or the twentieth-century definition: a term used originally by American sociologist P. A. Sorokin (c. 1937) to describe a type of culture based on spiritual values and ideals, whose material needs are the minimum necessary to forward those ideals." Indeed Betty's deployment of the term is resonant of "slippery" uses of words in Singaporean national rhetoric such as "garden city" and "heartland".

77 1982: paragraph continues.

78 1982: "regretted rejection".

79 1982: "of".

80 1982: "&".

81 1982: "the Art & the Science & the Philosophy". Paragraph continues.

82 The final sentence is a parodic reworking of Faustus's paean to Helen of Troy in Christopher Marlowe's *Doctor Faustus* (Scene 13, line 90 [A-text]).

"HIS LITTLE AREA OF ANIMATION":
AN ESSAY

READERS AND SCHOLARS of twentieth-century Singapore, Southeast Asian and postcolonial writing in English will be served well by this collection of Arthur Yap's eight short stories, published here together for the first time. Before this publication, these works remained under the radar of literary reception. Yet three of these eight stories appeared in *Singapore Short Stories* and have been studied as set texts for Literature at the GCE "O" Levels in 1991. In that same year, "Story of a Mask", was adapted into a drama and performed to 4,500 people, a number which even now is considered a success in audience outreach. I am undeservedly honored to be writing this essay, as I count myself among the scholars who had remained largely ignorant of Yap's short story production.

I first met Yap in 1982 when I was a visiting faculty member at the University of Singapore. He was quiet, polite, reclusive, and steadfastly unavailable socially. I did not find his diffidence strange—poets come in all shapes, and silence, exile and cunning (as James Joyce famously noted) are often the strategies for writers whose beliefs and passions are discordant with their (national) communities. Yap's adamant avoidance of the limelight may partly account for the comparative critical neglect of his work and his relative invisibility during most of his publishing years.

Yet Yap may not have been unhappy with this obscurity. In 1985–86, I spent a year at the Institute of Southeast Asian Studies (ISEAS) and decided to include Yap's oeuvre as a topic of research. After I had completed drafting a chapter on his work, I sent him a copy, requesting to interview him for a response. When we met at the ISEAS lounge, I vividly recall him being uncomfortable, almost disquieted by my critical attention. When I asked him about his ideas concerning the relation between the poet and society, the poem and the communal context in which it is embedded—the focus of my interpretations—he pointed me to his previous interview with Kevin Sullivan (noting that it made another interview with me unnecessary), and generally repeated the ideas expressed there (ideas of community that are also articulated in "Story of a Mask"). Yap did not press me for any revisions in the chapter or contest my readings; instead, he requested that I rethink my use of the term "subversion" in the chapter's title. I honored his request by changing the title to "Sub/Versions of a National Poetry".[1]

A sparse record of publication may explain the ignorance and neglect of Yap's prose fiction. Angus Whitehead's collection gathers together a total of eight short stories—some no more than two pages in length—beginning with two stories appearing in campus magazines in 1962 when Yap was nineteen. They all appear over a span of twenty years in small, local publications with little or no regional or international circulation. 1978 was a good year, when three stories were published. But this spurt of production was followed by four years of silence. The next story, "A Beginning and a Middle, without an Ending", which was published in 1982 and then revised and republished eleven years later, remains (as far as we know) his last attempt at short fiction. Set against canonical masters of the genre such as Anton Chekhov (over 200 stories), John Cheever (almost 200); closer to home, Gopal Baratham (five collections), Catherine Lim (nine), indeed Yap as a short story writer seems a slight figure. Slight as it is, however, this collection edited by Angus Whitehead forcefully highlights a number of attributes of Arthur Yap's literary production. For one, despite his reputation for writing inaccessible, minimalist poetry, "fiction" as storytelling is clearly a major structuring principle in his first genre of choice. And this imagination is populated with characters, actions, suspense, ironic themes, settings, social worlds, and what Bakhtin termed the "stylistics of dialogism", "heteroglossia", "polyglossia", and other discursive features that instate relations among language, interactions between subject and others, and shifting social constructions. Such a dialogic approach eminently illuminates the dynamic processes that underlie Singapore writing in English that is contextualized in, constructed by, and itself participates in and shapes a multilingual, multicultural and highly hybrid national character. At the same time, just as many of Yap's poems—once his fictionalizing drive has been clarified—will be re-read with a different edge—as dialogic productions—so these eight stories must be read in the context of his entire oeuvre as a writer, and as poetically constructed, devised through the rhetorical strategies of compression, indirection, imagism, symbolic action, and poetic devices such as allusion, alliteration, rhythm, and so forth.

Despite being produced over twenty years, these stories exhibit a fairly coherent core of interests, points-of-view, themes, and common

[1] See *Nationalism and Literature: Literature in English from the Philippines and Singapore* (Quezon City: New Day Publishers, 1993), p. 130-56

social worlds that demonstrate an evolution of a recognizable structure of feeling. From the first unnamed protagonist in "Noon at Five O'Clock," characters appear encumbered by communal cultural expectations, caught in the grip of social norms that hold no meaning for them. This vacuity of individual value in social relationships is reflected in a physical world that the subject finds hostile and is estranged from; this world offers no resource or access to transcendentalism, delight, or pleasure, except in fugitive moments or through accidental discovery. If transcendence, transformation, agency or meaningful actions are not to be enacted by the individual subject, and does not arrive from a *deus ex machina* or external actors, how then can the individual escape from these social claims, this emotionally vacant landscape? In many of the stories, instead of melodrama or drama, characters are drawn as if in portraits, through plotless moments. The stories suggest epiphanies that offer no transformation but some kind of re-cognition, and in that re-sighting some revelatory relief, resignation, and re-signification. Recognizably "Singapore" in descriptions of tropical heat, sociocultural references, overt statements, and allusions, the setting is hardly ever a territory that appeals to the senses and imagination. Place is an imagined construct, but one with few delights.

To this territorial imperative—the insistence on place and society as concrete, inescapable realities—the stories pose characters who seek and/or find furtive secret alterities in psychically charged subterranean and subterfuge sites. In this way, one may say that Yap's imagination is relentlessly anti-plot. From the very first published story, two words "plan" and "accident" emerge as antithetically linked, around which a plangent dualistic epistemology emerges more fully with each new story. Resisting the bureaucratically planned homes of the Housing and Development Board (HDB) in 1960s Singapore, the protagonist in "Noon at Five O'Clock" seeks/desires an alternative space: "there are always (to him rather delightful) accidents." An early poem expresses a similar insight in a similarly imagined moment:

> on a hot day I think
> everything is an accident ("hot day", *only lines*)

As a form of covert resistance to the new city/nation-building housing projects, the narrator-protagonist chooses "the oldest and creakiest-looking door" that opens symbolically to a past and its decays: the past is discoverable only as accident, unplanned for, serendipitous, but not in any reified or reductive manner. The delight has nothing to do with the desire to recreate ancestral identities or to recover a historical identity (the decrepit door "leave[s] the back to the family ghosts"). Stepping through that door, the character reveals that choosing the non-new is in fact not a choice in favour of looking back, a desire for the past, but a choice that is against the future as planned, a choice for the accidental that is not manipulated, predictable—an agency to be enjoyed privately ("But he didn't make a religion out of his OWN view. Which was why he enjoyed it"). This private preference is not to be to be declaimed, preached, shared, or collectivized. Yap's stake in an extreme privacy and determined anti-communal stance is already enunciated in this 1962 text.

This paradox may be the core of Yap's predicament as a prose writer: how to enunciate—itself a rhetorical challenge of public inscription if not communication—subjects set apart as private and individualized, while critically conscious that such claims to privacy and individuality—even as they openly disavow collective, social, and national significance—will nonetheless be read as part of that collective, national fabric? Does he pull back into silence, the ultimate privacy of the individual, or will he negotiate the difficult terrain between the private and the public, the individual and the social, the aesthetic and the ethical or political?.

Instead of resistance, "The 5-Year Plan", the second 1962 story, has two characters who accept the plan set out for them. They marry, have a child, and aspire to middle-class comforts and rank. Then the plan goes dreadfully awry. The husband incurs a gambling debt and the rest of the couple's lives are taken up with unremitting work to pay off the debt. There are no delightful accidents for the couple. The traditional plan is evacuated of meaningful life; the five-year plan to pay off the debt before moving on with one's desired life is endlessly deferred. The "5-Year Plan" becomes the literal meaning of their lives; debt slavery ensues. Reduced to work to pay off the debt, their lives finally become absent of meaning. Here, Yap's narrative voice is overtly satirical, speaking with a kind of cold cruelty and disciplined by an ironic distance in which the narrator remains separate from the characters and actions he portrays. The incremental estrangement of subjects from meaningful lives deny agency to these characters; their transformations occur with a strange passivity, without voluntary agency.

But Yap's stories are resistant to plots of victimization. These are not narratives of dramatic tragedies but elusive passages on lives of "quiet despair," without an Immanent Nature to retreat to. "The 5-Year Plan" scripts multiple losses, the chief being the loss of meaning: living in a condition where things, relationships, and actions no longer signify, except as these relationships and actions—narrativized in stories like "Soo Meng" (1970), "The Effect of a Good Dinner (1978) and "None the Wiser" (1978) —gesture to the social and ethical vacuum that yawns as a deadening boredom behind the surface of familial and communal niceties. These stories re-present a grim kind of realism with repressed dramatic violence, resulting in an apparent absence (because unacknowledged or unconscious) of strong sentiment, conflict, and interpersonal engagement. Tensions arise and are negotiated through collective epistemes, while the individual is muted, elusively drawn, a fugitive (in "Soo Meng", a mildly affected Down's Syndrome child, whose parents keep him near invisible, is killed in a car accident when he is finally let out into the community). Freedom, coming out, is preferred to enclosure and the social callousness of outcasting, but the same mobility carries dangers and social carelessness. In "The Effect of a Good Dinner", desire is acknowledged, but it must be collectively managed and diverted to regulateable and acceptable means and ends. The deployment of negative and double negatives in these stories is a form of indirection, as is the use of the impersonal voice:

> He was born an idiot. And why not? It wasn't his choice (etc.), that much is obvious. The main thing was that he didn't look like one, not by a wide grin [...] I suppose people have now learnt not to let things be, without having to resort to tears, without sneers" ("Soo Meng").

The late stories, being more developed, delineate more complex characters, while also expressing more empathetic identification. In "Story of a Mask" (1978), which is a re-working of aspects of the earlier "A Silly Little Story" (1964), Wong Loo, a Chinese opera actor from China, has made a place for himself in Singapore. Contrast this Singapore-identified artist with the earlier manifestation of Wong Loo in "A Silly Little Story", who, the narrative notes, is a diasporic Chinese rather than an assimilated Singaporean and who therefore would feel at home in any Chinatown in the West: "Wong Loo was just plain and simply tolerant, and that was perhaps his saving grace. Therefore, a lot of things, big and small, did not irk him at all." The reconceptualized Wong Loo in "Story of a Mask" emerges as a dynamic shifting construction of China and Singapore, past and present, individual and collective:

> They brought with them, among other things, their beliefs, their superstitions and folkways and, when they were unhurried (which was quite often), they looked around and saw that, though they felt unchanged, they were in fact changed [...] it was by recounting the things of the past that they were able to trace the differences between themselves then and themselves now.

The "Story of a Mask" is more fully developed than the six stories published before it; it is less indirect, more general statement, with greater ethnographic detail, and more narration, description, analysis, and rhetorical features associated with prose:

> Singapore prospered. And with greater purchasing ability people could now afford some culture. [...] Opera, given a kick, reared to its heyday. Permanent theatres were set up, notably the ones in the Great World, the New World and the Happy World. These Worlds, too, had changed.

Explicit, summative, general statements with a slight ironic edge—as in the style of social satire—cover spans of time and space economically. Increased purchasing power results in being able to "afford some culture"— the local relation between 'culture' and commoditization is lightly mocked here. The different "Worlds" (well-known amusement parks in Singapore) are punned with the world that these agents live in, where change is unpredictable and outside of monetary control.

This second Wong Loo is an actor who "played, unfailingly, the role of the hero" (the first Wong Loo's profession is unknown). The plot pivots on the traditions of the art of Chinese opera, in particular acting in a mask of white rice powder. Ironically perhaps, it is this masked actor who is given the power of loving the city he finds himself in—Singapore. Characters who are psychologically rather than literally masked are viewed as discredited in their expressions of loving sentiment. When Kok Lian asks his siblings in "None the Wiser" if one of them would take in their elderly mother,

Kok Beng answers, "I would love to have mother with us [...] but I don't think she'll take to Phyllis's cooking"; filial love is deployed ironically in the use of the conditional tense. Similarly, in "Story of a Mask", the author omnisciently notes that the audience "[i]nvariably [...] loved" the masked hero; with the intensifier "invariably" underlining the ironic interrogation of the sentiment. The story goes on to narrate that the public's love of both the masked hero and of Chinese opera is variable, depreciating with the years and social change. Only in the description of aspects of "Chinatown" as an analogue for traces of Chinese culture and values is love enunciated unironically. These vivid descriptions of Chinese artifacts and Chinatown ambience, which "seem frantically real," first appeared in "A Silly Little Story" ("the display of the sticky stalks of plum-flowers standing in big jugs of brine, and which are available only at the New Year season [...] the articles on display in the shops—the odd items in furniture, the brass joss stick containers, the miniature trees, the lacquer and the bamboo chopsticks") and are repeated in "Story of a Mask" almost verbatim.

When Wong Loo, exhausted after a performance, falls asleep without washing off his mask, the omniscient author slips into a mythological point-of-view—rare in Yap's poetry and fiction—thereby providing a dramatic denouement to the plot. The soul, not recognizing the body's masked face, is unable to return:

> The limp body was not familiar: it was slumped on the bench, but its face was not as usual. It was still and white, a mockery of the real thing.

> Next morning, they found him dead.

The last story, "A Beginning and a Middle Without an Ending", seems somewhat mistitled. Being the only Yap story where causality appears crucial in explaining and understanding character, it does have a plot and hence an ending. Yap can explore causality, in this rare Yap story with a plot, because the story investigates beneath the surface to the inner workings of people and events. Two sisters, Elaine and Betty, are seen in two scenes set years apart. In the first scene, the elder sister Elaine slaps Betty for acting out a faint to conclude her performance of a Taiwanese song that she is obsessed with because of the Taiwanese singer's dramatically emotional presentation. The singer's presentation, as with all good art, offered Betty an insight into a sensibility that was otherwise closed to her. In the second scene, set decades later, Betty is an executive of a company that selects and trains young women in the arts of self-presentation. This juxtaposition suggests that Betty's success is motivated by her sister's violent slap years earlier. Although Betty is now able to assist Elaine financially, the story shows her first reducing the sum she wants to give to her from a thousand to two hundred dollars, and finally tearing up the two hundred dollar cheque. The focus is on Betty, whose present character (calculating, controlled and controlling, emotionally withdrawn, and manipulative, all traits that make her a dominating and fearsome executive) the story seems to suggest, is a response to that formative moment, one for which Elaine remains un-forgiven.

However, perhaps the notion that the story has no ending may be to draw the reader's attention to a seeming indeterminacy in the story's actual conclusion, which offers Betty's interior conclusion:

> somehow, in between the chuckle and the choke, Betty Wong drew a conclusion. It was the collapse before the song started. And poor Elaine, the face, the recollection of the face that could not launch Betty Wong's hand.

That the younger sister enjoys holding the superior position to the elder is clear (Elaine is both economically and emotionally downtrodden). But how does Elaine's face fail to launch her sister's hand? Is this passage a restatement of Betty's refusal to send the cheque to Elaine (i.e., to come to her rescue as the Greeks did with Helen abducted to Troy)? Unlike the beautiful Helen, poor Elaine's remembered face fails to move Betty. But what collapse before the song does Betty recall? That the sibling rupture had occurred even before Betty's performance began? That it was actually sibling rivalry that motivated Elaine's violence on her sister and not the pretended faint that appeared to provoke Elaine's rebuking slap? In short, the concluding passage overthrows causality for character; the collapse between the two sisters occurs before the events of the narrative even occur. In brief, while the reader may infer causality from narrative action (plot), it is in fact relational characters that are the causal agents of the action. It is not action that leads to character, but character that leads to action.

The last story confirms a major but subtle theme in Yap's stories: socially constricted characters are so not because of systemic structures and circumstances that appear to shape them but because they are intrinsically shallow, ungenerous, afraid, competitive, ignorant, submissive, weak, and more. The Singapore society Yap's stories intuit is often critically drawn as emotionally muted, because the individual characters he inhabits the city with are muted. Lee Kok Liang, a member of an earlier generation of Malayan/Singapore fiction, called these Chinese immigrant-natives "mutes in the sun" (*Mutes in the Sun*, 1974). Yap's minimalist prose is another stylistic tracing of this particular trope of the diasporic Chinese community. These small, selfish, despairing, struggling, cruel protagonists emerge as themselves, because as Shakespeare said it, "The fault [...] is not in our stars, But in ourselves, that we are the underlings" (*Julius Caesar* 1.2.140–1).

Shirley Geok-lin Lim
Research Professor
University of California, Santa Barbara

This essay is from chapter 5 of Arthur Yap's *a brief critical
survey of prose writings in Singapore and Malaysia* (1970)

Short Stories

SHORT STORIES have not attained the popularity that novels have. One
reason is that, until recently, there have been few short story writers—or, to
put in another way, there are many short stories but few short story writers
proper. Most of these stories are undergraduate attempts. Hence, until one
comes to the 60s, one is inclined more to talk of short stories than of short
story writers.

Another reason for the lack of popularity is that of the narrow
scope offered. Writers could adapt historical facts for purposes of
fiction, but this has been done often enough and yet it is in novels that
one finds this. One example is Harun Aminurrashid's *A Malay among the
Portuguese*. Moreover, with the increasing tempo of life and the search
for more concrete and salient features for representation, it is not often
that writers look into events of the past. On the other hand, writers have,
and are, attempting to represent our ways of life within the span of a
short story. But in doing this, the difficulty is one of scope. Communist
indoctrination, inter-racial marriage, the War and its aftermath, tradition
and the insurgence of modernity are the key themes. In a novel, any one
of these topics can be treated fully. A short story usually offers insufficient
room. Consequently, it appears as an ad hoc piece of writing if it is written
more to push a point rather than to let the story tell itself. This can also
result in stilted presentation, especially when local expressions are not
inherently incorporated.

The 1950s, and particularly the 60s, see the emergence of a greater
and more articulate attempt in making the short story more substantial in
assimilating the locale and life here. This is seen also in Donald Moore's
The Sacrifice and other Stories (1957), a collection of competent stories,
although the title-story itself runs in a rather facile manner on a popular
theme—that of Chinese-educated students who become Communist-
minded through youthful zeal and a blind sense of loyalty to China. The
advantage of this collection is that the writer is fluent.

The lack of fluency is seen in some of the stories in *The Compact*, edited by Herman Hochstadt (1959), and Part One of *Bunga Emas* edited by T. Wignesan (1964). There are fifteen stories in *The Compact* and they are, variously, stories of unrequited love, such as Lloyd Fernando's "Twixt cup and lip"; episodes, such as Balan Sundram's "A Saturday Night"; stories of the attainment of adult awareness, such as Awang Kedua's "A New Sensation"; and stories which are fabricated on a 'heavy' issue, such as Tan Hock Seng's "The Compact".

Those in *Bunga Emas* are by S. Rajaratnam, Lee Kok Liang, Awang Kedua, Ooi Boon Seng and T. Wignesan. Many of the stories in both collections, though this is less true of these in *Bunga Emas*, suffer from an awkwardness in presentation. The presentation in Tan Hock Seng's "The Compact" and "You Cannot Live", for instance, is rather elephant-footed and is unable to sustain the line of argument. And unless the ideas are either startling or profound enough, it is unlikely that the story can be expected to be borne solely by the weight of the ideas alone.

On the other hand, Awang Kedua's "A New Sensation" and the stories by Lee Kok Liang are eloquent, and enlist the reader's attention fully. This is due to a greater skill of presentation and in letting the story unfold itself, without having to become turgidly moralistic or to lapse into question-begging.

Lee Kok Liang has also a collection of his short stories published under the title of *Mutes in the Sun and other Stories* (1964). There are eight satisfying stories, with the title-story occupying nearly half the book. Kok Liang manages a subtle ring of irony. Sometimes, there is also a tinge of the macabre, as in "Five Fingers"; but the attempt in this story is not successful as it gives a rather portentous affectation to the tone. "Just A Girl", "Mutes in the Sun", and "The Glittering Game" show the writer's acumen and perception and, while it may be said that he attempts at being stylistic; these stories are strong enough to withstand even occasional lapses of style.

The following passage from "Birthday" shows his restrained and subtle style:

> Grandmother was talking, asking about the fruit plantation Uncle Teng had, how many coconuts he got per tree, and whether the white ants were giving trouble, and if they were he should go to the 'redhaired' man's store and get some liquid. If he did not

have enough money, she would lend him some.

While saying this, Grandmother smiled at her. Uncle Teng nodded and also smiled.[1]

Grandmother was trying to match-make the girl in question; she was trying to ascertain Uncle Teng's financial position and to offer some considerate advice.

The North Borneo Literature Bureau has brought out several publications, among which are J. M. Chin's *The Nyonya* (1962) and *The Santubong Affair* (1964). Both are extended short stories dealing with the subject of parentage—the first, that of a young man's discovery, through reading a diary that his deceased aunt kept, that she was really his mother; the second, the motivation for Gilbert Lee's revenge upon a wealthy businessman is that the latter is his father. He was the man who seduced his widowed mother. The woman died after giving birth to a son — Gilbert. The second story is in the nature of a not very gripping who-done-it. On the whole, both make easy reading. The writer's interest is with people in certain situations and this topic is surely appealing enough if it is well presented.

In the same year, the North Borneo Literature Bureau put out Tales by Lamplight, a collection of four stories. The first, "Tales By Lamplight" by Joan Craen, is a series of episodes told, as the writer remembers, by the Grandmother. It has the flavour of a children's story and is attractive in its way. "Poonek" and "Tricked Again" by Lim Beng Hap are stories that are well worth a reading.

An outstanding book of short stories is Choo Soon Yin's *Shadows of Evening* (1964). The nine stories are of the Japanese Occupation. Three of them, "And Women Must Weep", "Camouflage" and "Vain Shadows", form a trio of stories about the hardships and incidents encountered by a family, the Ko family. The other stories are also about the Japanese Occupation and its aftermath. "The Wheel Of Fate", an attempt at oblique narrative is a brilliant story told with a sureness of touch. "The Nightmare" and "In The Swirling Current", stories of shady Japanese M.P.'s are also successful. All in all, the stories are skilfully constructed and, despite an occasional euphuism, they are told in a manner devoid of the special pleadings that can come so easily in stories of such a topic.

[1] Lee Kok Liang, *Mutes in The Sun,* Rayirath 1963, p. 31.

Twenty-Two Malaysian Stories, selected and edited by Lloyd Fernando (1968), is a collection that justifies the editor's belief that these stories offer some evidence of an adaptation of English "to the fresh outlook that is the making in Southeast Asia". Seven of these stories are by Lee Kok Liang; one of them, "Ibrahim Something" ends with this paragraph:

> I stayed on in the hospital for a few more days but did not talk much to anyone. Ibrahim left the evening his brother died, although he was still unwell, and the last I heard was that he had slipped into the jungle with the guerillas, taking his wife with him. That's what the people said. For all that he might be tending a patch of vegetables near the edge of the jungle, for our country was still big and lonely enough for people like Ibrahim and his wife to live their own lives without dreams.[2]

"Ibrahim Something" is a well-integrated story. There is nothing hypothetical about the theme or the characters. In coming to its conclusion, the reader is not forced to look past Ibrahim's ears to watch the writer grappling with a problem he only intended to leave to the participants. It is clear that the commitment is resolved at the end of the story as the writer feels and understands his subject-matter.

[2] *Twenty-Two Malaysian Stories*, selected and edited by Lloyd Fernando, Heinemann Educational Books 1968, p. 228.

Year	Events	Publication	Painting
1943	Born at River Valley road		
1945			
c. 1954–60	Attends St Andrew's School	Early poems published in the St Andrew's school annual	
1961–5	Attends University of Singapore. Taught English Literature by D. J. Enright	Three short stories, numerous poems and a critical essay published in *Focus*, the literary magazine of the University of Singapore	
1967	Works as a Pre-University English Literature teacher at the Serangoon Gardens English School March–April: Participates in poetry festival, Centre 65.		Begins painting

1968	March: Takes part in an "Evening of Poetry and Folk Music", the National Theatre Club Auditorium	Poem "A Scroll Painting" published in *New Voices of the Commonwealth* (London)	Paints "Evening (Petang)"
1969			Paints "Isorhythm I", "Untitled (Blue and Green)", and "Untitled (Green and Orange Waves)" First solo art exhibition, featuring 44 square abstract paintings, at the National Library at Stamford Road
1970		Short story and poems published in anthology *The Flowering Tree*, ed. Edwin Thumboo Publication of *a brief critical survey of prose writings in singapore and malaysia*	Paints "Untitled (Vermillion and Blue)" Second solo art show held at the Lecture Hall of the National Library

1971		February: Five Star Gallery opens at Liat Towers with a year-long exhibition including Yap's paintings
1972		Yap's paintings represent Singapore at the Adelaide Festival of Arts
1973	Poetry published in *Seven Poets*, ed. Edwin Thumboo	Paints "Untitled (Blue Composition)" October: Solo exhibition entitled "Lyricisms 1973" held at the Alpha Gallery, Alexandra Avenue
1974	Yap's poetry published in anthology *Five Takes*	June: Solo exhibition of acrylic paintings, created between 1969 and 1974, held at the Alpha Gallery
1974–5	Pursues an MA in Linguistics and English Language Teaching at the University of Leeds, England	Paints "Black and White Series", 1–17

1976	Pursues a PhD in Linguistics at the University of Singapore	Poems published in *The Second Tongue*, ed. Edwin Thumboo
	Receives National Book Development Council Award for Poetry for *only lines*	
1977	May: Takes part in "An Evening of Poetry and Music", the National Museum		Paints "Early Evening"
1978	October: Asserts in *Straits Times* that standards should be set to encourage and promote local writing	Three of Yap's short stories included in *Singapore Short Stories*, ed. Robert Yeo
1979	August: Takes part in "An Evening of Poetry and Music", Regional English Language Centre, Orange Grove Road, and reads a selection of Wong May's poems	
1979–98	Works as lecturer in linguistics at National University of Singapore	

1980	Begins co-editing *Singa* with Kirpal Singh and Sng Boh Khim		Paints "Untitled", "Landscape", "Landscape II", and "Untitled II"
	February: Takes part in a forum-cum-exhibition on local writing, National Library		"A Small Complete View I", "Landscape Situation II", and "Overland"
	April: Reads poems at "Singapore: Past and Present", Raffles Hotel		
1982	Receives PhD in Linguistics	"A Beginning and a Middle Without an Ending" first published in Malaysian literary journal *Tenggara*	Paints "Brown Landscape"
	September: Receives National Book Development Council Award for Poetry for *down the line*		
1983	Receives South-East Asia Writers Award in Bangkok from Thailand's Queen Sirikit	Poems published in National University of Singapore Literary Society's publication *Focus* (1983)	
	Receives Cultural Medallion for Literature		

1984	October: Reads at "A Lunchtime Poetry Reading", the Shell Theatrette, Raffles Place	Paints "Window View" June: Works exhibited at Alpha Gallery and National Museum Art Gallery
1986	Publishes his final collection of poems *man snake apple* at his own expense	Poetry published in *The Poetry of Singapore*, ed. Edwin Thumboo et al.
1987	November: Reads at "Yin Yang" Festival, the Guild House at the University of Singapore	
1988	Receives National Book Development Council Award for Poetry for *man snake apple*	October: Yap's recollection of his childhood, "Of Green Men and Macho Beef", published in *Straits Times*
1991	Yap's three stories included in *Singapore Short Stories* are studied as set texts for Literature GCE "O" Levels June: a dramatized version of Yap's	

	"Story of a Mask" performed in over 14 performances to 4,500 people, mainly schoolchildren	
1992–6	Appointed a mentor with the Ministry of Education's Creative Arts Programme	
1993		Revised version of "A Beginning and a Middle Without an End" published in *S. E. Asia Writes Back!*, ed. C. Y. Loh and I. K. Ong
1995	Selected as one of five poets studied for Literature GCE "O'" Level.	
1996	Initial diagnosis of laryngeal cancer	
1998	Together with Catherine Lim, receives Montblanc-NUS Centre for the Arts Literary Award for English Literature	Rajeev Patke, a colleague at the National University of Singapore, records Arthur Yap and other local poets reading their poetry

2000	Cancer in remission	Publication of selcted poems, *the space of city trees*	Exchanges works with Ho Chee Lick, fellow local artist and friend. Yap's painting given to Ho is featured on the cover of this book.
2001			
2004	Return of cancer, removal of voicebox		
2006	19 June: Passes away		
2007	November: Yap's life and career celebrated at Singapore Writers Festival		
2008	11 July: Reading and exhibition held in honour of Yap		Boey Kim Cheng writes essay on Arthur Yap's painting, which will be published in Gui Weihsin, ed. *Common Lines and City Spaces* (ISEAS, 2014)
2009		Poems published in the Norton poetry anthology *Language for a New Century*	

2010		Yap family donates some of his paintings to the National Gallery Archives, Singapore
2013	National Arts Council commissions Royston Tan to direct short film based partly on poem "2 mothers at a h d b playground"	Publication of *The Collected Poems of Arthur Yap* (NUS Press)

"Poetry and Folk Music Concert", *The Straits Times*, 15 March 1968, p. 4.

"Art Show", *The Straits Times*, 18 November 1970, p. 6.

"Art Gallery Opening", *The Straits Times*, 1 February 1971, p. 9.

"New Paintings on Display", *The Straits Times*, 15 October 1973, p. 9.

"One Man Show", *The Straits Times*, 14 June 1974, p. 7.

"Evening of Poetry at Museum", *The Straits Times*, 3 May 1977, p. 7.

Choo Wai Hong, "Dearth of Quality Stories in English: Editors", *The Straits Times*, 19 October 1978, p. 8.

"An Evening of Poetry and Music", *The Straits Times*, 30 August 1979, p. 2.

Koh Juan Toong, "A Collage of Poetry and Song", *The Straits Times*, 7 September 1979, p. 3.

Lena Bandara, "Getting to Know Our Writers;...He's Come a Long Way from those Rhyming Lines in the School Mag", *Sunday Times*, 4 November 1979, p. 1.

Arthur Yap, "Spontaneous Verses of Child Poets Mirrored in Magazine", *The Straits Times*, 25 May 1980, p. 1.

Nalla Tan, "Spontaneous Feeling that Comes Right from the Heart" [appreciation of Yap's *down the line*] *The Straits Times*, 6 July 1980, p. 8.

Gillian Pow-Chong, "He Holds Up Mirrors", *The Straits Times*, 30 May 1982, p. 2.

"Journal Looking for Local Literary Talent", *The Straits Times*, 28 January 1983, p. 18.

Anthony Burgess, "Too Much Eliot and Alas, No Ulysses", *The Straits Times*, 9 August 1983, p. 8.

"S'porean Writer Honoured with Award in Thailand", *Singapore Monitor* (Afternoon Edition), 31 October 1983, p. 8.

Yeow Mei Sin, "Poet's Success Story", *Singapore Monitor*, 11 November 1983, p. 8.

Rebecca Chua, "Arthur and His Art", *The Straits Times*, 14 November 1983, p. 1.

Francis Ong, "They Made S'pore Culturally Richer", *The Straits Times*, 17 November 1983, p. 1.

"Poetry Reading", *The Straits Times*, 21 November 1987, p. 3.

Mary Rajkumar, "Of Green Men and Macho Beef", *The Straits Times*, 11 October 1988, p. 1.

Koh Buck Song, "A Step in The Right Direction", *The Straits Times*, 27 December 1989, p. 3.

"No, No, We Don't Mean Singa the Courtesy Lion", *The Straits Times*, 20 June 1990, p. 26.

"S'pore Short Stories a Sell-Out", *The Straits Times*, 15 June 1991, p. 24.

"You're All Write, Here Is A Pen", *The Straits Times*, 3 October 1998, p. 3.

Helmi Yusof, "Poetry Between Mutter and Stutter", *The Straits Times*, 19 February 2000, p. 16.

Aaron Lee, "Poetic God of Small Things", *The Straits Times*, 4 March 2000, p. 20.

Ong Sor Fern, "Arthur Yap", *The Straits Times*, 12 February 2001, p. 2.

———. "A Man Of Few Words", *The Straits Times*, 21 June 2006, p. 2.

Janadas Devan, "Pared Down Poet", *The Straits Times*, 25 June 2006, p. 24.

Cheong Suk-Wai, "For Better Or Verse", *The Straits Times*, 6 July 2006, p. 6.

Adeline Chia, "Painting Another Picture of Poet Arthur Yap", *The Straits Times*, 30 November 2007, p. 88.

————."Voice of Arthur Yap", *The Straits Times*, 6 December 2007, p. 75.

Stephanie Yap, "A Private Person; Poet of the Interior", *The Straits Times*, 6 April 2008, p. 70.

Trevor Tan, "An Artist's Masterstroke for Cancer Research" *Today*, 12 July 2008, p. 8.

Stephanie Yap, "10 Poets Make Norton Cut", *The Straits Times* (Afternoon Edition), 18 January 2009, p. 68.

Yap, Arthur, *only lines*. Kuala Lumpur: Federal Publications, 1971.

————. *a brief critical survey of prose writings in singapore and malaysia*.
   Singapore: Educational Publications Bureau, 1971.

————. *commonplace*. Singapore: Heinemann Asia, 1977.

————. *down the line*. Singapore: Heinemann Asia, 1980

————. *man snake apple and other poems*. Singapore: Heinemann Asia, 1986.

————. *Thematic Structure in Poetic Discourse*, Singapore: Copinter
   Publications, 1987.

————. *the space of city trees: selected poems*. London: Skoob Books, 2000.

————. *The Collected Poems of Arthur Yap*. Singapore: NUS Press, 2013.

ARTHUR YAP IS one of Singapore's most important poets. He published four major collections of poetry: *only lines* (1971), *commonplace* (1977), *down the line* (1980), and *man snake apple & other poems* (1986). Of these four, *only lines*, *down the line*, and *man snake apple & other poems* all won the National Book Development Council award for poetry.

He also contributed a section of poetry to *Five Takes* (1974), a publication featuring Chung Yee Chong, Sng Boh Khim, Yeo Bock Cheng, and Robert Yeo. Other awards included the Southeast Asian Writers Award (1983) and the Montblanc-National University of Singapore Center for the Arts Literary Award for English (1998).

Known also as a painter, Arthur Yap held exhibitions locally and abroad. In 1983, he was awarded the Cultural Medallion for his contributions to literature in Singapore, and from 1992 to 1996, he served as a creative writing mentor for the Creative Arts Program under the aegis of the Ministry of Education. Arthur Yap obtained his PhD in Linguistics from the National University of Singapore in 1982, and taught at the Department of English Language and Literature there until 1998. He passed away in 2006 at the age of 63.

ANGUS WHITEHEAD is Assistant Professor at the National Institute of Education (Nanyang Technological University) in Singapore. He is currently completing a monograph on the later and posthumous lives of William and Catherine Blake.

SHIRLEY GEOK-LIN LIM is Professor of English at University of California, Santa Barbara. She is also a well-known poet and writer, and has penned several books including *Monsoon History: Selected Poems* (1994) and *What the Fortune Teller Didn't Say* (1998).

RAJEEV S. PATKE is Director of the Division of Humanities at the Yale-NUS College. His research interests include Modernist literature, poetry and painting, and the works of Walter Benjamin.